THE ITALIAN
BILLIONAIRE'S
RUTHLESS
REVENGE

Lincolnshire
COUNTY COUNCIL

Working for a better future

discover libraries
This book should be returned on or before the due date.

3 0 SEP 2017

To renew or order library books please telephone 01522 782010
or visit https://lincolnshirespydus.co.uk
You will require a Personal Identification Number
Ask any member of staff for this.
The above does not apply to Reader's Group Collection Stock.

EC. 199 (LIBS): RS/L5/19

£13.50

L 5/9

THE ITALIAN BILLIONAIRE'S RUTHLESS REVENGE

BY

JACQUELINE BAIRD

™MILLS & BOON®

Pure reading pleasure

First published in Great Britain 2007
Large Print edition 2008
Harlequin Mills & Boon Limited,
Eton House, 18-24 Paradise Road,
Richmond, Surrey TW9 1SR

© Jacqueline Baird 2007

ISBN: 978 0 263 20042 3

Set in Times Roman 16¾ on 20 pt.
16-0508-54217

Printed and bound in Great Britain
by Antony Rowe Ltd, Chippenham, Wiltshire

CHAPTER ONE

THE gleaming black yacht cut swiftly through the green waters of the Mediterranean Sea, slowing as it approached the island of Majorca to berth perfectly alongside the marina at Alcudia. With a satisfied smile, Guido Barberi handed the wheel back to the Captain.

'I'll leave the rest to you.'

Wearing only white shorts and soft shoes, he walked out onto the deck. He cast a fleeting glance at the bustling tourist-filled waterfront of Alcudia town, before turning his attention to the crew as they secured the ship to its mooring. Satisfied everything was secure, he let his dark gaze wander admiringly over the classic old yacht berthed alongside his. It stayed. His tall frame tensed as his eyes narrowed intently on the two women sunbathing on the timber deck.

One, a blonde, was sitting up and watching the arrival of his yacht with obvious interest. But it was the other one, lying flat on her stomach on a sunbed, who captured his attention and made every predatory male sense he possessed leap to instant attention.

It could not possibly be her, he told himself. But the compulsion to make sure was overwhelming. Slowly he lifted the binoculars strung around his neck to his eyes, and focused on the prone female. From the soles of her feet his gaze trailed slowly up long, shapely legs to a small pert bottom, and he drew in a stunned breath.

They were there…nestled near the base of her spine…two perfectly formed circular dimples. Swiftly he looked up the length of her body, noting the slender indentation of her waist, the smooth shoulders and the rich golden-brown hair haphazardly looped in a knot at the back of her head. She was reading a book, oblivious of his scrutiny. His firm mouth twisted in a grim smile as his dark gaze slid back down the length of her spine again.

Only once had he ever seen a woman…*known*

a woman… who had such distinctive dimples in just that place. The kind that had totally fascinated him. The kind his lips had touched and his tongue had teased countless times before he eventually possessed her hot, welcoming body. He let the binoculars fall and shoved his hand in the pocket of his shorts as his body reacted with lightning-fast enthusiasm at the thought.

It had to be her. It was her. His ex-wife. Sara Beecham.

Memories he had thought long-forgotten came rushing back.

Even now he could still remember the exact moment he'd set eyes on her. She'd had her back to him, and the low-slung hipster jeans she'd been wearing had just covered her delightful bottom, but had fallen short of meeting her top by a good nine inches, revealing the two dimples that had totally intrigued him. When she'd turned around her beauty had taken his breath away, and the well-filled short sweater, tiny waist and long legs had turned him on so fiercely he hadn't dared move. It had been love at first sight—or so he had thought at the time.

In hindsight he realised it had been sheer unbridled lust on his part.

But his brief marriage had been an education in the faithlessness of women, and of this one in particular. As soon as his back was turned she had left him, clutching the cheque she had demanded from his father. He had returned home to find his bride gone—no sign of her remaining except a short note wishing him farewell. He, fool that he was, had refused to believe it. But a quarter of a million pounds cashed within days of her return to the UK had managed to convince him. The divorce had been handled swiftly by the lawyers and he had never seen her again until today.

'Will you look at *Il Leonessa*? Now, that is what I call a yacht. I think it's the new Predator class. Wow! Never mind the ship—what about the man? Look… *Look*… Oh, my God. Isn't he just the most gorgeous hunk of masculinity you ever saw? Look at those shoulders, that chest, the legs…'

Sara felt the dig in her ribs and reluctantly tore her attention away from the tale of murder most foul she was reading. She cast a sidelong glance at her companion.

'Oh, please, Pat—not another Greek god stepped down from Olympus. He must be about the hundredth you have spotted in the past week.' She grinned. 'And you a married lady.'

'Believe me, this one is exceptional. Unless he has rolled-up socks stuck down his shorts, he has to be the best-looking, most rampantly virile male I have ever seen. Unfortunately he's focused on you.' Pat sighed ruefully. 'Still, I bet he's great in bed.'

'You are disgraceful.' Sara shook her head and returned to her book.

'And you, girl, are wasting your life. You're on a yacht with six single men and only two female guests. It's perfectly obvious Peter Wells has the hots for you, and do you encourage him? No. When you're not cooking you spend most of your free time with your head buried in a book. Where is your spirit of adventure? If I were you I would be straight over there and trying to find out who that beautiful man is. In fact, I think I will anyway. I'll invite him to our farewell party tonight. Dave won't mind if I tell him he's for you.'

'No.' Sara spun over and sat up. 'Don't you dare.' But she was talking to her friend's back. The trouble was Pat *did* dare…anything. And Dave, her husband, was just as bad… Initially, as their sometime accountant and friend, Sara had tried to teach them the benefit of restraint. But the word was not in their vocabulary.

So Sara had answered Pat's frantic telephone call to ditch her own holiday, get down to Marseilles and join their cruise as the cook. The one they had hired had failed to turn up and they'd been desperate. Having shared her apartment with Pat when she'd first started work with an international accountancy firm in London, Sara knew how useless Pat was in the kitchen. Sara knew without conceit that she was an excellent cook. She also knew just how perilous their financial situation was.

On their marriage three years ago they had both given up their jobs and sunk all their money, and some more besides, into this yacht—the idea being to make a living from running cruises with an element of training people to sail when they were not sailing off somewhere themselves. It had sounded good on paper, but with Pat now pregnant they would shortly need somewhere to live—preferably back in England. Dave confidently expected to keep the yacht, and rent a place in London until the baby was born and able to sail with them. But Sara had seen the figures, and knew how horrendously expensive it was simply to own the yacht.

The trouble was, although it was a decent size with four guest cabins, the ship was quite old. A stunning timber-built sailing cruiser, it was very romantic to see in full sail, but very expensive to maintain and run. Even with Dave as instructor and certified captain and Pat as crew, the bare minimum they could sail with was three qualified sailors plus a cook and a cabin boy—and their wages had to be paid. As for the insurance, it was colossal to cover the yacht and the paying guests. Sara knew because she had arranged the policy for them.

The charters tended to be groups of young people who had experience of sailing and liked the idea of learning more. But they were on an expensive holiday, and if the wind dropped and it looked as if they might miss a single port of call they expected the engine to be utilised. Given the astronomical rise in the cost of fuel over the last two years, calm seas could virtually wipe out any profit on a charter. Plus, simply keeping it berthed in the Mediterranean accrued very hefty fees—which was why Sara had given up the second week of the Cordon Bleu cookery course she had been attending in the South of France to help them out.

Sara glanced up idly at the much bigger vessel opposite. Good Lord, it actually had a helicopter on the top deck. Heaven knew what kind of money it took to run a ship like that…millions, probably, she thought, her gaze skimming down.

Then she saw the object of Pat's enthusiasm—or at least the rear view of him. He was tall, with black hair, wide shoulders and a broad back tapering to a lean waist and hips and long, muscular legs, and he was about to enter the wheelhouse. Great body, she thought, and then inexplicably she shuddered. Someone walking over her grave. She shrugged and, rolling over on her stomach, was soon lost in the intricacies of a very bloody murder case.

Later that evening Guido Barberi leant against the rail of the neighbouring yacht and studied the woman who had just appeared on deck. If anything the last ten years had increased her beauty, Guido thought dispassionately. Her long chestnut hair fell in casual waves over her shoulders and her silken skin was lightly tanned to a soft golden glow. Her perfectly arched eyebrows framed dark thick-lashed blue eyes, her nose was small and straight, and the top lip of her luscious mouth formed a natural cupid's bow. She was wearing a white wraparound dress in a fine fabric that revealed the soft swell of her firm, obviously braless breasts. It emphasised her tiny waist and ended a few inches above her knees to reveal long legs. On her feet she wore jewelled flip-flops.

He felt an instant stirring in his groin and his mind was made up. It was over two weeks since he had finished with Mai Kim in Hong Kong and returned to Italy. He had spent a few days at the family home in Naples, to attend his younger brother Aldo's wedding, and then left to take delivery of his new yacht in Monaco. Two days ago he had sailed from France with the representative from the yachtmakers' and his new crew to put the yacht through its paces. Satisfied everything was in order, he had sailed on at a leisurely pace this morning for the island of Majorca. He had been enjoying the peace and relaxation he thought he needed, which the yacht provided, but now he realised he needed a woman a whole lot more. One particular woman. And *Dio*, she certainly owed him, he thought, a bitter smile twisting his firm lips.

Sara stepped out onto the deck and grimaced at the crowd milling around in the limited space. As usual Pat had managed to swell the eight guests from England who had chartered the yacht to thirty or so. Why was she surprised? Pat had done the same at every port they had visited, intent on making the charter a success, hoping for a return booking from the group. It was good fun, Sara supposed, but truth to tell she was glad the cruise was almost over. They were sailing on to Ibiza tomorrow morning, and Sara was flying back home tomorrow night. This hectic lifestyle was not really her…seven days of sailing and partying was more than enough. Much as she loved cooking, after feeding fifteen people for a week, with only a cabin boy to help, she was all cooked out.

Still, she had no right to complain. In between ports and preparing meals she had caught up on her reading and enjoyed the company of the guests. In fact the change had done her good. She was feeling more relaxed than she had in years. Perhaps Pat was right… All work and no play was not good for anybody. And maybe it *was* time she found herself a man.

'Sara, you look fabulous as usual. Dance with me?'

'Peter.' She grinned at the tall blond man smiling down at her. He was employed by a top hedge fund in the City of London, as were all the guests, and he was viewed as something of a whiz-kid by the others. *Kid* being the operative word. He was only twenty-four, but had apparently already made a million in bonuses, and was in line for a lot more. He worked hard and played hard…

'Is there enough room?' she queried, eyeing the few square metres of crowded deck, and then added, 'Yes, why not?' as she moved smoothly into his arms. 'It's our last night, so you can't possibly get up to any more tricks here,' she scolded him with a reminiscent smile as they moved easily to the music.

So far he had made her miss the tender back to the yacht when they were anchored off Corsica, snatched the top of her bikini from under her when she was innocently lying on her stomach reading a book on a beach in Sardinia and tried to get her drunk countless times. And yesterday he had thrown her overboard off the island of Minorca, then made a drama of rescuing her—despite the fact that, as a strong swimmer, she had not needed rescuing.

'Oh, I don't know…' His arm tightened around her waist, and before she knew what he intended a large hand grasped the base of her neck and his laughing mouth covered hers. She was so astounded she did not try to resist, and a moment later she acknowledged he was no *kid* when it came to kissing!

Lifting his blond head, he grinned, his blue eyes sparkling with merriment and something else. 'I was determined to kiss you before the end of the cruise to let you know what you are missing,' he declared outrageously.

Her own lips curved in a rueful grin. The kiss had surprised her, and it had been very pleasurable—stirring her blood a little for the first time in years. And, yes—Peter was right—it had reminded her of what she had been missing. But it was the *something else* that bothered her. Held close to his muscular torso, she could not help but be aware of his aroused state and, planting her hands firmly on his broad chest, she pushed out of his arms.

'It was even better than I imagined.'

'Well, in future stick to your imagination,' she said dryly. 'Because I am not looking for a toy boy.' They had become good friends over the last week, and she did not want to offend him, but she was not sure she wanted to encourage him on the strength of one pleasurable kiss. Though, far from disgusting her, she found his instant arousal rather flattering. Maybe after ten years of celibacy her body was trying to tell her something, and it might not be such a bad idea…?

'Ah—you cut me to the *quick*!' he exclaimed, with a hand on his heart.

Sara chuckled. Peter really was irrepressible… Handsome, with boundless confidence, he had girls falling at his feet and he knew it. Had she ever been that young and carefree? she asked herself, before quickly dismissing the thought. Tonight she was going to enjoy herself. The yacht was strung with fairy lights, the chatter of the crowd was friendly and the music and laughter created a near perfect ambience.

'I have never understood exactly what the *quick* is.' She grinned up at Peter. 'And you, sir, are a drama queen.'

'You know me so well, dear heart.'

'God—you are so over the top I'm amazed any girl ever falls for it.'

They laughed in mutual accord.

'Come on.' He flung a friendly arm around her shoulder. 'I'll get you a drink.'

She cast him a sidelong sardonic glance.

'And, no, I am not going to try and get you drunk. But you do look hot—really hot…'

He smiled lasciviously.

'Majorca in June *is* hot, and it looks like being a stifling night,' she said glibly, ignoring his innuendo.

Guido's lips curled in distaste as the fair-haired guy took his ex-wife in his arms. Why was he surprised? He had done some checking after Pat Smeaton had boldly boarded his yacht and introduced herself before inviting him to the party.

Pat and Dave Smeaton owned the yacht. Smeaton captained the vessel, and apparently— with the help of his wife and four crew—he ran it as a business. They took groups of people on private cruises. The present guests were all employees of a highly successful hedge fund run by a business acquaintance of Guido's—Mark Hanlom. Apparently the fair-haired man was Peter Wells, the golden boy. But Sara Beecham, as she was now known—having reverted to her maiden name—was not employed by Hanlom. Watching her dancing with the young man, Guido had a pretty good idea why *she* was on board.

He straightened from the rail and stepped forward, his lithe body stiffening in outrage as the couple holding his attention kissed. His dark eyes flared with rage, and it took every atom of control he possessed not to push through the dancers and rip the woman from the guy's arms.

Guido was shocked rigid by his own reaction. He hadn't thought of his ex-wife in years. A host of other women had kept him quite satisfied in the sexual department, and if he had thought of Sara at all it was with contempt, as a greedy, heartless little bitch. His eyes rested on her.

He watched the laughing, friendly banter between the couple, and when the boy flung his arm around her shoulder and led her towards the bar he drew in a harsh breath. Sara—his ex-wife—the woman who had once carried his child—was not even aware of his presence…

It was a new experience for Guido. He was not conceited, but he knew he was usually the object of every female's eyes wherever he went. Yet Sara had not noticed him… Or had she?

Over the last decade Guido had seen every trick in the female arsenal used to capture his attention. Maybe she was playing games? *Dio!* She was an expert at it, as he knew to his cost…

But not this time. Straightening his shoulders, and with the lithe grace of a panther stalking his prey, he moved swiftly through the crowd to where the bar had been set up and stopped a foot behind her.

'Sara.' He drawled her name and placed a hand on her bare shoulder. 'It *is* you, Sara?' he queried in mock surprise.

'I know you,' the young man blurted over Sara's head. 'You're Guido Barberi, the legendary transport tycoon and wizard financier.' Holding out his hand, he added, 'Peter Wells… great to meet you.'

Guido took the offered hand when really he would have liked to knock the younger man flat on his back. This guy was obviously a good friend of Sara's. He even had the audacity to kiss his ex-wife in public, and heaven knew how much more.

Yet he appeared to regard *him* with the respect due a superior. Legendary, for hell's sake!

'The pleasure is all mine,' Guido responded briefly, and let his dark gaze drop to the woman who was staring up at him as if she had seen a ghost. 'But it is Sara I wanted to speak to. We are old friends. Aren't we, Sara?' he demanded silkily.

CHAPTER TWO

THE moment she heard the deep, dark voice drawling her name Sara had known it was him... Guido Barberi... She had whipped round, dislodging his hand from her shoulder, her entire body tensing in instant defence against the long-forgotten sensations that just the sound of his deep, slightly accented voice aroused, and now she gazed up at him in total shock.

For a long moment she simply goggled at him like an idiot, unable to believe her eyes. He was here, in the flesh, all six feet two of him, towering over her. Guido...her ex-husband.

He was casually but impeccably dressed, in a short-sleeved shirt open at the neck to reveal the strong column of his throat. Casual linen pants hung low on his hips, supported by a leather belt slipped through the loops, its buckle a discreet silver rectangle resting on his flat belly... No, she wasn't going any lower...

Abruptly she lifted her head, her blue eyes roaming over his face. His black hair was cut shorter, now with a side parting and a few wayward curls edging his broad brow. He was still darkly handsome, but not in the youthful way she remembered. His chiselled features had somehow hardened. The high slant of his cheek-bones was more pronounced, a few telltale wrinkles creased the corners of his black eyes and the firm, sensuous lips were held in a tight line. Hard and obviously successful, he exuded an aura of power and confidence that few men could hope to match. And she had personal ex-perience of how ruthlessly determined he could be in using every one of his considerable array of talents to get what he wanted.

She gazed up at him, numb with shock. She opened her mouth to say something, but her mind was in turmoil, a host of conflicting emotions swirling inside her.

'Sara.' He said her name again. 'Surely you have not forgotten me?'

She saw the mocking amusement in his eyes and knew he was deliberately baiting her. Anger, swift and piercing, brought heightened colour to her pale cheeks. He had made a fool of her once, made her life hell, but never again. She was twenty-eight, not eighteen any more, and she had moved on.

At twenty-five she had got the opportunity to buy a partnership in a long-established Greenwich accountancy firm, Thompson and Son. The reason being that Sam Thompson, getting on in years, was the 'Son', and he had wanted a partner basically so he could cut down on work and play more golf. The business was now thriving. Sara was successful in her own right, and she did not need this heartless, arrogant swine looking down on her.

'Of course not, Guido. But where did you come from?' she demanded. Realising how dumb the question sounded, she did not wait for an answer. 'And as we have not met in almost ten years I think *old friend* is a bit of a stretch,' she tagged on in a remarkably cool voice, given that inside she was shaking like a leaf.

'My yacht is berthed opposite, and a rather lovely blonde invited me.'

What an appalling coincidence. Sara almost groaned out loud. That floating palace was *his*, and Pat had invited him… She shouldn't be surprised. When had he ever refused the offer of a beautiful woman? The first time she had met him he had been attending a party as the date of an older student who had lived in the same block of apartments as Sara, and yet he had flirted and walked off with Sara—and she had been besotted enough to let him.

In fairness to the other girl, the next day she *had* tried to warn her. She had told Sara he had picked her up when she was with another man, that he was a consummate seducer of women and not to be trusted for anything other than a brief fling. With hindsight Sara wished she had taken note of the girl's warning instead of putting it down to jealousy. Her blue eyes shadowed briefly with remembered pain and more…

Suddenly aware of the lengthening silence, Sara belatedly responded with, 'I see.' And finally she *did* see the past clearly.

Guido had been her first and only lover, and when she'd got pregnant and he'd married her she had thought life could not be more perfect. When he had taken her to Italy to live with his family in a huge villa set on the Bay of Naples she had realised he was quite wealthy, but it hadn't bothered her. In the end a lethal combination of his family's hateful attitude towards her, Guido's impatient dismissal of everything she tried to tell him, as well as his obvious lack of trust in her, had nearly destroyed her.

She had had no choice but to leave to save her sanity.

Looking now at the incredible yacht he owned, and recalling a feature article a glossy magazine had done on his life when he had turned thirty, she knew she had never been in his class. The article had catalogued his life from school to university to running the family trucking firm. Through his brilliant financial acumen Guido Barberi had managed to transform the business, with the acquisition of a fleet of container ships, oil tankers, a cargo airline, and many other diverse companies, into one of

Italy's most successful conglomerates. From a single freight company in Naples the Barberi Group had grown into one of Italy's most profitable firms, employing more than two hundred thousand people across the world.

'The Barberi Group—Moving the World' had been the headline for the article. As for Guido Barberi, it had said he was considered one of the most eligible bachelors in the world, and the number of beautiful women he had dated was too many to mention. But there had been no mention of him ever being married.

He had airbrushed Sara out of his life with the same ruthless efficiency with which he had got rid of her. She supposed he might have married in the four years since the article. Caterina had tolerated his womanising playboy lifestyle, but surely even *she* must have put her foot down eventually?

Her blue eyes studied the handsome face that still had the power to make her pulse race. But now she also saw the ruthlessness in the smile that never reached his predatory black eyes. This was a man confident in his masculinity, with an inbuilt arrogant belief in his supremacy over lesser mortals—a man few, if any, would dare defy. And she knew she had made the right decision all those years ago.

Guido saw a flicker of what looked like fear in her blue eyes, and the slight dilation of her pupils she could not disguise. He had felt the tremble of her silken flesh beneath his hand when he had touched her. His dark gaze dropped to where her breasts pushed against the fabric of her dress, the taut outline of her nipples clearly visible, and a sense of elation soared through him. She might not have been aware of him when she had first appeared on deck, but she sure as hell was now. Her body betrayed her— just as it had years ago, when they'd first met.

Turning his attention to Wells, he drawled, 'I'm sure you won't mind if I claim this dance with Sara? We have a lot of catching up to do.' He watched the confusion on the younger man's face, then lowered his gaze to Sara, a challenge in his dark eyes.

Much to Sara's relief, at that moment Pat

appeared and grasped Guido's arm. Her relief was short-lived.

'Great, Guido—you're here. Let me introduce you around. First this is Sara Beecham, our chef. Do me a favour and use your charm—which I know you have in abundance—and try and get her to enjoy herself.'

'I am well ahead of you,' Guido responded—with his usual smooth charm, Sara thought bitterly. 'I have already asked Sara to dance, and am waiting for her answer.'

'Of course she will,' Pat said blithely, responding for her, and then added, 'Go on, Sara. I have told you over and over again, you are in danger of becoming a stereotypical cook—eating your own food and getting fat.'

'Thanks, Pat.' Sara shot her friend a furious glance. They had agreed at the start of the cruise to preserve the professionalism of the yacht venture—Sara would refrain from telling anyone she was really an accountant. But *fat*…

Pat would pay for that later, Sara vowed, but contented herself with saying, 'I can speak for myself.'

A moment later Guido's hand was on her back and he was urging her out onto the small deck.

Out of the frying pan into the fire, Sara thought helplessly, instantly aware that the pleasurable sensation Peter's embrace had surprisingly aroused increased a thousandfold when Guido turned her to face him. The hand at her back encircled her waist, to pull her closer to his tall, lithe frame, the other hand stroking up her spine to splay across her back between her shoulderblades.

She stiffened in his hold, fighting against the old familiar sensations his touch evoked, and it was just her bad luck that the music changed to a slow number. More likely Pat had purposely changed the CD, she thought angrily.

She put her hands on his shirtfront to hold him at bay. There was nowhere else to put them unless she laid them on his dark, slightly hair-dusted forearms. And she did not want to touch his naked flesh...too many memories... She glanced up at him and for a moment imagined she saw a venomous glint in his dark eyes. But she must have been mistaken. His firm lips had parted in a slow smile.

'So you're a cook? That does surprise me—though maybe not,' he amended. 'Given your supposedly fragile state when you left me I guess university was too much for you. Then again, the quarter of a million you got from my father must have been burning a hole in your pocket. I expect you had a ball until the money ran out,' he drawled sardonically.

She had to bite her tongue to stop herself revealing the truth. Any lingering doubt about Guido's knowledge and approval of his father's actions in chasing her out of Italy was finally dispelled, and the slight guilt she had felt at keeping the money was banished once and for all.

'Yes, I did,' she lied.

There was no way she was revealing the agony she had suffered at the loss of their child and at his complete indifference to her feelings during their mercifully brief marriage. And she thanked the Lord her honorary sister Lillian had stopped her ripping the cheque in half and bullied her into banking it.

That money had enabled her to resume her accountancy degree and buy a small flat in

London. Then later, along with a small legacy she had received from her mother's estate, it had allowed her to buy her partnership in what was now Thompson and Beecham Accountants Ltd in Greenwich. She had sold her flat in central London, and with the help of a mortgage had bought a two-bedroomed apartment overlooking the Thames in Greenwich, within walking distance of her office. Life was good, and she was not going to let meeting Guido again upset her. So she looked up into his hard, dark eyes and simply added, 'And I like cooking.'

'As I remember you were a good cook, among other things, when we first met and married.' She saw the blatantly sensual gleam in his eyes and knew exactly what he meant. She had been his willing slave, in bed and out. 'Though you quickly lost interest once we moved to Italy.'

Ignoring the sexual connotation of his words, she concentrated on the rest. 'Funny—I seem to remember your parents already had a chef.' He had conveniently forgotten that, living with his family, she had not been allowed in the kitchen— if he had ever noticed! But trust him to twist things around to suit himself, she thought, bitterness and anger welling up inside her.

'And with your mother, aunt and cousin Caterina taking over when the chef was absent I wasn't needed,' she reminded him bluntly. With Caterina around she had not been needed for anything—not even as his wife. Though for a brief few weeks she had been tolerated because of her pregnancy. The familiar stab of pain at the thought of the child she had lost made her stiffen even more in his arms—if that was possible.

'It was a casual comment of no import.' Guido shrugged, recognising her simmering anger and remembering all too well her paranoid dislike of his cousin. Not that it mattered now. He wanted to bed Sara, not take her anywhere near his family. He changed the subject. 'Relax, Sara, and let's enjoy a dance as old friends should.'

Had they ever been friends? Sara silently questioned. Lovers—yes, and husband and wife for a brief time, but they had actually spent barely six months together, and almost half of that had been an absolute disaster... She had been married at eighteen and divorced at nineteen. But the memory of that catastrophic year still had the power to hurt her.

'You're remarkably silent, and yet I seem to remember you used to be quite the opposite— very talkative.'

'Yes, well…as I said, I was surprised to see you,' Sara managed to respond firmly. 'I thought you would be married again with a few children by now.'

'And how do you know I am not?' he queried mockingly.

'I don't, and I am not really interested; I was simply making polite conversation,' she said curtly. Their own marriage had not stopped him leaving her at the mercy of his family in Italy while he took off to America, and she doubted the intervening years and another wife would have changed him. Once a rat, always a rat…

'Well, I am not. Once was more than enough for me,' he stated, and tightened his hold on her waist.

Sara felt the brush of his muscular thighs against her own, and every nerve in her body screamed in outrage. At least she told herself it was outrage.

Because the alternative was too humiliating to contemplate. 'Me too,' she agreed adamantly.

'It is good we can agree on something.' He smiled—a brief twist of his firm lips. 'Maybe we should pursue the subject and discover what else we have in common after all this time?' He paused, his hot, dark eyes capturing hers as he drew her closer. 'I have never forgotten the sexual pleasure we shared, *cara mia.*'

Her mouth fell open in utter astonishment at the endearment, and the seemingly idle stroking of his thumb against her back sent a shudder down her spine. Oh, *no*, she thought frantically, recognising the sudden electric awareness in every cell of her body as an uncontrollable physical response to a man she had every reason to hate. How was that possible? she wondered helplessly, unable to tear her gaze away from his, the air between them positively crackling with sexual tension.

'We were so good together,' he murmured. He was so close she could inhale his scent, and the warmth of his breath made her skin prickle with awareness. 'And we could be again.'

'In your dreams,' she fired back, but heat suffused every inch of her skin—a heat that had nothing to do with the stifling evening air.

'No.' He smiled and crooked an eyebrow at her. 'Dreams are fantasy… Good sex is reality. Be honest, Sara, the sex between us was always spectacular, and the chemistry is still there.'

He wanted her, and for a second she actually felt flattered—until she recalled his callous indifference to everything that had happened between them before. She swallowed the lump of misery that rose in her throat. 'You are just the same. Sex is all you ever wanted from me.'

'Still do.' A small smile curved the corners of his incredibly sensual lips as his arms tightened around her, the hard muscles beneath his shirt pressing against her sensitive breasts. She glimpsed the intent in his heavy-lidded dark eyes a second before he lowered his mouth to hers. Her mind screamed *no* but as his tongue slid effortlessly between her parted lips her body refused to listen.

It was how Sara imagined being swept up in a tornado must feel. The heat, the sensations like a primitive force of nature battering her, spiralling around her, sweeping her higher and higher until she was flung back in time, lost in the splendour of their first passionate embrace.

The persuasive movement of his tongue, skilfully exploring the moist interior of her mouth, and the warmth of his hand, sliding up her back to tangle in her hair and deepen the kiss, were unleashing emotions she was helpless to control. Sensual longing raced like wildfire along Sara's veins, melting what little resistance she could muster, and her body quivered in eager response. The movement of his other hand slipping to cup her bottom and urge her into the powerful strength of his thighs was so familiar and, oh, so right…

He crushed her to him and without missing a beat manoeuvred her in time with the music, his mouth never leaving hers. Her mind went blank to everything except the memory of how often they had danced like this, felt like this, loved like this. It was as if all the power of her sexuality that she had kept suppressed for so long now surged into vibrant life. Of her own accord her hands on his chest swept up to clasp his broad shoulders, and she surrendered hungrily to the sensual delight of his kiss and kissed him back.

She whimpered as he drew his mouth back a little, then moaned as his teeth bit lightly on her swollen lower lip, wanting more.

'This is far too public,' he murmured, his lips trailing a line of fire from her mouth to her ear. 'Follow my lead.'

She trembled as his long leg eased between hers and his strong hand exerted the slightest pressure on her hip to guide her backwards.

Suddenly he stopped and released her, and, deprived of his support, Sara swayed helplessly. She felt a wall against her back and, gazing dazedly around, found they had moved to the seaward side of the yacht, shadowed from the decorative lights strung around the deck.

'Not perfect, but better,' Guido whispered, and lightly brushed her lips with his own, before trailing a line of kisses down her throat.

Sara sighed, lost in a sensual dream of the past. She felt his palms cup her breasts, his fingers squeezing her straining nipples over the fabric of her dress, and, pliant, she curved against him. She was drowning in a stormy sea of exquisite sensations, and didn't notice when his hands deftly untied her dress.

When he raised his dark head her thick lashes slowly fluttered upwards to see him looking down at her, molten desire swirling in the depths of his night-black eyes. She reached for him.

'No—first let me look,' he husked, and slowly unfolded her dress to leave her revealed in only tiny lace briefs. 'If anything you are more incredibly beautiful than I remembered.'

All Sara could do was look up at him with glowing eyes, every atom in her body crying out for his possession. It had been so long since she had felt the touch, savoured the scent of a man…this man…

His hand reached for her, his fingers stroking over the soft curve of her breast and cupping its swelling fullness.

'*Dio*, I need to taste you.' She heard him groan, and then he was suckling her breasts with a teasing, torturous pleasure that made her arch against him. A hand stroked up her thigh to cup between her legs and she shuddered, aching for a far more intimate touch.

'You really are so hot. So sexy,' he rasped.

His dark head lifted and Sara's wildly dilated blue eyes met his. She saw the passion, the desire in his hard, handsome face, saw him lean back a little, his eyes flicking lower to the rigid peaks of her naked breasts. She felt a slight cool breeze against her overheated skin.

'I want you, Sara—very badly. But I need to know. Has Wells already been here today?'

Sara felt his hand flex between her legs as his huskily uttered words sank into her dazed mind. The reality, the horror of her situation hit her with the force of a thunderbolt…

And she hit him.

Instinctively her hand formed a fist and she punched him square on the jaw, with a perfect uppercut, taking him completely by surprise. She saw him stagger back against the guardrail. Pity he hadn't fallen overboard…but drowning was too good for the bastard. His type should be hung, drawn and quartered, she thought furiously as she pushed past him and wrapped her dress swiftly back around her trembling body, tying the knot firmly around her waist.

A long arm latched around her waist before she had taken two steps, and she was spun around, her back flat against the wall again. Her knuckles were hurting, her heart pounding, and she had trouble believing she had just punched him. Her brief foray into boxing as a means of keeping fit had not been wasted after all, the irreverent thought popped into her head. But one glance up at the man looming over her, his big body taut, his dark eyes blazing with fury, and suddenly she no longer felt quite so brave.

'What the hell was that for?'

His hand shot out and roughly tilted her face, so she was forced to look into the pitch-black depths of his eyes. She saw the fury, the passion, and she dragged in a ragged breath, her heart pounding as he raged on.

'You were with me all the way. You were gagging for it,' he snarled. 'So what changed, you crazy bitch? Have you lost all sense? A lesser man might very well have hit you straight back.'

It was the *crazy bitch* that did it…

Bitter fury engulfed her, and something more. Her slender body froze all lingering traces of arousal stone-dead, and the blue eyes that stared into his were icy with contempt.

'You dare to ask me what changed? After you had the gall to ask me if you were going to be my first lover of the day?' She shook her head in disgust, dislodging his hand from her chin. 'You ask me if I have just left one man's bed for another's? In my book a man cannot get much lower than that.'

Guido Barberi—tall, dark, handsome man of the world, sophisticated and experienced lover, powerful financial tycoon—felt a wave of heat wash up over his face that had nothing to do with sex. And for the first time in his thirty-four years he blushed as the import of her words struck home.

Had he actually asked Sara such a gauche, insulting question? Yes, he had, and for a brief instant he was embarrassed. Another first for him. He glanced down at her, his dark eyes narrowing as they met cool blue and then roamed over the beautiful face framed by a tumbling mass of chestnut hair. The white dress was back in place and she looked almost virginal… But he knew better. He should—he had taken her virginity. And that was the problem, his analytical mind reasoned.

The blue-eyed little witch had always had the power to tie him up in sexual knots. He had never known a hotter lover—not before or since Sara. She had the uncanny ability to turn him on faster than the speed of light. Some things never changed and seeing her again today had been one hell of a shock. Watching her kiss and flirt with the young man, naturally he had reacted possessively. It had simply been a throwback to the past, and that was why the stupid question had popped into his head at the worst possible time.

'If I was tactless then I apologise,' he said harshly. 'It was juvenile, maybe, but it was not unreasonable—given you were kissing the boy ten minutes before me.'

'You have never been juvenile in your life, Guido, and if that is your idea of an apology, forget it.' And, dipping under his arm, she dashed back towards the stern.

CHAPTER THREE

SARA jerked to a stop as a long arm circled her waist once more, and she threw back her head, ready to do battle.

'Oh, it's you…' She was relieved to see Peter, and grabbed his other arm to help steady her trembling legs as the aftershock of what had occurred struck her.

'I was looking for you…'

'Get me that drink you promised,' she demanded breathlessly. 'I certainly need it.'

He glanced over her head, and back at her. 'I can see why. Your old friend does not look too pleased.' His concerned eyes smiled down into hers as he urged her towards the bar. 'Are you okay?' he asked, after picking up two glasses of champagne and handing one to her.

'Yes—yes, fine now.' And after taking a long swallow she added, 'Thank you.'

'No need for thanks. I'm your knight errant, don't you know? But I have a nasty suspicion that is all I will ever be. Without wishing to be insulting, you have the look of a woman who has been thoroughly kissed—unfortunately not by me,' he said wryly. 'But to heal my bruised heart you have to come clean and tell me how you know Barberi—and why the man has just given me a guns-drawn, shoot-at-ten-paces look.'

Sara knew she owed Peter some kind of explanation. 'I met him years ago, when I was a teenager at university. I knew him for a few months, and then we went our separate ways.' She had no intention of going into detail.

'Let me guess… You left him? I am right, aren't I?' Sara nodded her head in agreement. 'That would account for the filthy look.' He chuckled. 'Guido Barberi is a man no woman turns down. They always chase him, and he has dated some very lovely ladies.'

'I can imagine.' Sara snorted disgustedly.

'Not the half, I bet. The man is a legend in financial circles. His base is in Italy, where it's rumoured a model amuses him. He recently opened an office in London, but he also has one in New York, to oversee his North American interests, where his lawyer there, Margot James, is his lover. I don't know about his South American and African offices but I know for a fact a few weeks ago he was at his Hong Kong office, where a cute Chinese girl called Mai Kim is his mistress. I was there on business myself, and saw them together. So hats off to you, Sara. I think you had a very lucky escape. You are far too exquisitely unique to be one of a harem.'

Her blue eyes misted with tears. There were some decent men in the world after all, Sara thought, and lifted her hand to stroke his cheek in a friendly gesture. 'Peter, I think that is the nicest thing any man has ever said to me.'

'Hey, don't go all soppy on me, pal. Let's go and eat some of your fabulous food,' he suggested, and, taking her glass, he closed his arm comfortably around her and led her into the main salon, where Sara had laid out the buffet earlier.

* * *

Guido had instinctively stepped forward to follow her, but stopped. Damn it to hell! What was he doing, chasing after his ex-wife? She had quite openly admitted she had enjoyed spending his money, she'd had absolutely no shame, and the last thing he needed was to get involved with her again. Then he saw Wells appear and slide an arm around her. The other man's eyes flicked to his, and quickly away.

He didn't blame the boy for taking his chance with Sara—though the way he felt at the moment he wanted to strangle someone. The depths of his passion surprised even himself, and his hands clenched around the guardrail, his knuckles white with the effort to control the anger consuming him.

His big body still throbbed with frustration, and it took all the considerable will-power he possessed to regain his usual cool control and think clearly.

Sara had not changed; she was still after money, out for the main chance. She had led him on with her sexy body, her throaty moans, and then thought better of it, he reasoned cynically, when she had re-evaluated. Having conned him once, her chance of doing so again was nil...obviously the young Wells was a much easier mark.

Good luck to him. He didn't care, he told himself. Let the young idiot find out for himself what a scheming little gold-digger she was. Guido straightened and with a shrug of his broad shoulders walked back into the crowd. In minutes he was surrounded by three very willing females. He was spoilt for choice...

Sara was in the past, and that was where she would stay, and for the next half-hour he concentrated his attention on his very charming companions. Then he allowed his hostess to guide him to the buffet, where he was surprised to see Sara replenishing the dishes. He shrugged his shoulders. Why was he surprised? She was a cook, and what better way to hook a rich man than to work on a yacht? he thought contemptuously.

Later, back on deck, if his gaze strayed once or twice to Sara in the arms of Wells it was totally unintentional, and with his superior wisdom he told himself he almost felt sorry for the guy. By all accounts the young man was on the way to making a fortune and a brilliant career beckoned. It seemed a shame to let a woman like Sara get her claws into him, Guido mused.

By the time he left the party his mind was made up. In the interest of male solidarity it was his duty to save young Wells from Sara Beecham's clutches.

How, he had yet to decide. Though the rather interesting conversation he had shared with Pat and Dave, after he had made a point of seeking the couple out and thanking them for a pleasant evening before leaving, had given him an idea. An idea that was a win-win situation for him…

He would save a clever young man from making a bad mistake, promote his career and get him out of the way at the same time. With a bit of luck he would get the sexy Sara back in his bed until he had finally sated himself in her luscious body, and then he would walk away from her without a second thought.

* * *

Sara cast one last glance around the galley. The debris of the buffet had been disposed of and the place was spotless.

'There you are.' Pat entered as she was about to leave.

'If you have come to help—too late. I'm finished,' Sara said dryly.

'You bet you are,' Pat declared, grinning all over her face. 'You will never guess what... When I told Guido Barberi we were leaving tomorrow, about noon, he insisted on returning my hospitality of this evening by inviting everyone to breakfast on his yacht in the morning. Isn't that great?'

'If it means I don't have to cook and don't have to go...yes.'

Except when Pat finally left Sara felt anything but great. Gutted would be a more accurate description. Closing the galley door behind her, she made her way to her cabin, one of three in the lower deck of the yacht, designated for the crew. A quick shower, and she climbed naked into the bottom bunk. What a hellish night! She groaned and closed her eyes, hoping to blot out every

minute of the horrendous party, but to no avail…
Meeting Guido again had awakened a host of
memories she had struggled for years to forget.

Who had once said be careful what you wish
for in case you get it? Sara wondered, lying
wide awake in her bunk. Whoever it was, they
were right.

Born and brought up in London by a mother
who'd loved her and a grandfather who'd adored
her, she had had a happy childhood. She had never
missed having a father. Her mother Anne—a re-
searcher for the BBC—had explained that the
only man she had ever loved had died in a motor-
cycle accident a month before they were due to
marry. But as the years went by she had longed for
a child. So at the age of thirty-five, and with the
encouragement of her best friends Lisa and Tom,
who had been married for years but childless, all
three had decided on treatment. They went to
America on an extended vacation and whilst Lisa
and Tom underwent IVF treatment, her mother
tried artificial insemination. As she had explained
to Sara, in her case it had been successful, and Sara

had been the result. But unfortunately Lisa had not been so lucky and never had got pregnant.

With the innocence of a child, Sara had never thought anything about her birth. For the first few years of her life every weekend and holiday had been spent at her grandfather's retirement bungalow by the sea in Southampton. With her mother and grandfather for support, plus her honorary Aunt Lisa and Uncle Tom, she had grown up to be a bright, trusting child. Her grandfather had died when she was eight, and it had been a big loss to both her and her mother, but an even bigger loss had been losing her mother at the age of eleven.

Then the full import of her unusual birth had been brought home to her in a devastating fashion. The couple her mother had named in her will as Sara's guardians, if anything happened to her—Aunt Lisa and Uncle Tom—had been killed in the same car crash as her mother. The three of them had been to the theatre and on the journey home had been hit by a drunken driver. Distraught at the death of her mother, Lisa and Tom, Sara had found herself without a friend or a relative in the world. The flat she had shared with her mother had been sold by the lawyers, and after all the expenses had been paid a modest amount of money had been put in a trust for Sara until she was twenty-one. And Sara had been put in the care of Social Services.

Just thinking about the children's home they'd placed her in even now made her shudder. Nowadays children were housed in small groups of six or so, in modern buildings, but at that time, and because of her age, she had ended up with thirty other children in a grim old Victorian building with iron bars on the windows to prevent the more unruly occupants from escaping. Naively, when asked by an older girl about her parents, she had told the truth and revealed she was a donor child. Immediately she had been taunted by the other children. Jibes like, 'Your father could be a serial killer,' had been commonplace, or speculation that she might end up marrying her brother had been another favourite.

For months she had lived in grief and fear, hardly daring to sleep at night, and not surprisingly all her confidence drained from her. It had only been when she was introduced to Lillian Brown that she had slowly begun to recover. For the next few years she had lived in various foster homes until she went to university, and Lillian Brown had been the only constant in her life.

A remarkable woman, at twenty-nine she had been single and an international lawyer, hoping to make partner in her firm. She'd hoped one day to have a husband and family of her own, but in the meantime had joined a "Big Sister" scheme run by the authorities to take out a child who was in a care home or fostered for a weekend once every two to four weeks, sometimes longer. Lillian had been Sara's salvation. A bright, articulate woman, she'd restored Sara's confidence and self-esteem, and encouraged her to do well at school. She'd been a comfort, a mentor and a friend. It was thanks to Lillian that by the time Sara went to university she was a bright confident young woman.

She had loved university life, and when Sara had met Guido Barberi, near the end of her first year, she had thought life could not be more perfect. It had been sheer bad luck that Lillian had been handling a long drawn-out corporate case in Australia at the time. If Lillian had been around maybe she would not have been such a fool…

Sara stirred restlessly on the bunk. She could remember the moment she met Guido to this day…

A strange prickling on her neck had made her turn around, and she had looked up into a pair of dark smiling eyes and blushed scarlet. He'd been older than the male students she'd usually mixed with, and the most incredibly handsome man she had ever seen. When he'd spoken to her and asked her to dance in a deep, slightly accented voice she had been lost.

He'd taken her into his arms, his luminous black eyes had smiled down into hers, and she had fallen madly and deeply in love with him on the spot. When he'd moved her to the music she had willingly followed his lead. She would have followed him to the ends of the earth if he had asked. When he'd taken her home and kissed her goodnight she'd felt as if every atom in her body was about to explode, and for the first time in her life she had felt the overwhelming power of passion. He had asked if he could take her out to dinner the next night, and of course she had said yes. Seven days later she had walked into his apartment and into his bed. It had never crossed her mind to refuse him. Guido had been the love of her life.

More fool her! Sara thought, twisting restlessly in the narrow bunk. She didn't want to think about the tender, gentle passion with which he had initiated her into sex. Or the wild, passionate creature she had very quickly become in his arms as he had skilfully taught her how varied making love could be.

No... She buried her head in the pillow, her body burning with long-denied sensations. The best sex in the world could not make up for losing one's identity, and that was what had very nearly happened to her.

At first when she'd discovered she was pregnant she had been afraid, but Guido had calmed her fears and insisted on marrying her— which she had taken as proof of his love, though he had never actually said the words. She had existed in an ecstatic bubble of love. His response to the unconventional method of her birth had been to say, 'Your mother must have been a very brave woman with a great capacity for love, just like you,' and kissed her. She was convinced he was her soul mate. She had told him almost everything about herself, and she'd thought he had done the same. She'd known his parents lived in Naples, with his younger brother Aldo, and she had known his dad ran the family freight business—which she had imagined was a few trucks.

She had also known that Guido had worked for his father for a couple of years between university and coming to London, and that he wasn't mad keen on rejoining his dad full-time in the family firm—he'd wanted to make his own mark on the world. But she had gathered they were a close-knit family, and he loved them. Just the kind of family Sara had dreamt of during the years she was in care—and the kind of family she wanted to have with Guido and their child.

When Guido had been called back to Naples

she had thought nothing of it, quite happy to go wherever he led. His father had been ill; it was natural he would want his eldest son at home to help run the business. But when they'd gone to live with his family her bubble had very quickly deflated and finally burst.

His mother was an attractive woman, but as she did not speak English and Sara did not speak much Italian conversation between them had been limited. Still, Sara had thought she was rather nice. But his father had been nowhere near as nice. A tall, broad bull of a man, he was obviously the boss of the house, and had made it very plain to Sara that he was not pleased that his eldest son had married without his knowledge. He'd claimed that this was the origin of his illness—a mild heart attack—had only tolerated her because she was pregnant and useful to bear the next generation of Barberis. When Guido had explained about her lack of family, his casual revelation that she was a donor child and his father's barbed comments, had touched on scars still sensitive enough to hear an echo from the children's home that had judged her birth as less than natural.

But it had been the presence in the house of Guido's Aunt Anna—his father's half-sister, who had been widowed years ago—and her daughter Caterina, both of whom Guido had failed to mention, that had finally destroyed Sara's blind belief in her husband. Eventually destroyed her belief in love altogether. The deliriously happy pregnant young girl who had arrived in Naples as a newly-wed had returned to England ten weeks later a broken-hearted, frightened and bitterly disillusioned woman.

Again, Lillian Brown had been her salvation. When Sara had returned to London, homeless, it was Lillian who had taken her in—Lillian who had taken control and dealt with the quickie divorce. She had tried to convince Sara to demand a settlement, but Sara had flatly refused. She'd simply wanted the whole sorry mess over with.

A sad, wry smile twisted Sara's lips. Her brief sojourn in Naples as Guido's wife had been hell, but she had learnt one lesson: never again to be embarrassed by the circumstances of her birth. If the Barberi family were a classic example of a so-called normal family, then she was damn glad her mother had opted for a donor.

For deviousness, deceit and outright lying, not to forget threats and intimidation, the Barberi family would have given the notorious Borgias of Italian history a run for their money...

Thank God she would never have to see Guido Barberi again. By this time tomorrow night she would be home. And on that reassuring thought she closed her eyes and sought the oblivion of sleep.

Sara slowly opened her eyes, yawned, and stretched as the first rays of the morning sun gleamed through the small porthole. She had not slept well. Her dreams—or to be more accurate her nightmares—had been haunted by a tall dark man imprisoning her in his arms, possessing her with a passion she could not escape however hard she tried.

Sighing, she rolled off the bunk. The heat was already stifling in the tiny cabin—and, worse, the heat of her nightmares still lingered in her wilful body.

She staggered to the tiny shower and, turning on the water, let it rush over her naked flesh, relishing the cool spray. As the cold water refreshed her she mulled over meeting Guido again, and by the time she had shampooed her hair and stepped out of the shower she was her normal practical self again.

So it had been an appalling coincidence—but not a disaster. Though what had possessed her to let Guido kiss her and touch her last night she had no idea. She must have been mad—a temporary brainstorm, perhaps. She certainly did not love him any more—hadn't for years… In fact she felt nothing but contempt for the arrogant, womanising swine who thought he was God's gift to women.

She ignored the irrepressible voice in her head that said in the sexual stakes he surely was, and five minutes later, dressed in white shorts and a blue tee shirt, made her way to the galley.

With the water on to make coffee, she strolled out on to the deck. This was her favourite time of day, before anyone else was up, and she glanced around the seashore. The town without the tourists was quite picturesque, and it crossed her mind to take a stroll ashore. But, catching a movement on the yacht alongside, she quickly changed her mind.

Heading back to the galley, she thanked God she was going home tonight. Thirty minutes and two cups of coffee later she was joined by the cabin boy and three crewmen. With a few words in her schoolgirl French she quickly established that like her, they had no intention of going to Guido's yacht—they didn't imagine for a moment they were invited—and set about making their breakfast.

Sara served coffee to a lot of bleary-eyed people in the next half-hour, and despite Pat and Dave's entreaties flatly refused to accompany them when they finally left with the guests to breakfast on *Il Leonessa*.

Glad they had gone, Sara heaved a sigh of relief, and in moments had the galley shipshape again. Then, returning to her cabin, she packed up all her belongings—with the exception of a linen trouser suit and top to wear for her flight home. She swept her almost dry hair back in a ponytail and picked up her purse. An hour in town was what she needed—and a bit of retail therapy.

She bought a rather nice pair of shoes in one shop, and a postcard to send to no longer Lillian Brown, but Lillian McRae, and now living in Australia with her husband and two children. Seeing Guido again had reminded Sara of Lillian trying to advise her over countless long-distance telephone calls against rushing into marriage. If only she had listened. She stopped for a coffee and wrote the card, then posted it as she wandered back past the harbour to where a long sandy beach stretched around the huge bay.

Kicking off her shoes, she paddled along the waterline, feeling relaxed for the first time since she had set eyes on Guido again. She watched the hotels and cafés slowly come to life, and the tourists wandering out onto the beach with their children. One man trudged by weighed down with all the paraphernalia apparently necessary to keep his wife and three children happy, bringing a smile to her face. He was carrying a folding seat and a huge beach bag, but it was a big green inflatable crocodile which seemed to have a life of its own that was giving him the most trouble.

He saw her smile and simply laughed. She couldn't help thinking wistfully that his wife was a lucky woman...

She glanced at her watch. Almost eleven—time she made her way back, as they were leaving at noon. She paused for a moment, her sandals in her hand, and looked out to sea. She let the gentle waves wash over her feet one last time and then, tightening her grip on the shopping bag in her other hand, she turned.

'Good morning, Sara.'

Sara sucked in a shocked breath. Guido stood in front to her, tall, dark and stunningly handsome, with his firm lips parted in a brilliant smile.

'Here—let me take that.' And before she could recover from the shock of seeing him again a large hand reached out and took the shopping from her unresisting one.

'No—it's okay,' she said, but too late.

'Rubbish. It's the least I can do for my ex-wife,' he stated with a grin. His dark eyes swept down over her scantily clad figure in blatant masculine appreciation, pausing to linger on her braless breasts, clearly outlined beneath the soft cotton of her tee shirt, before returning to her face. 'Though I would like to do a lot more. With your hair in a ponytail and wearing those shorts you look as young and beautiful as when we first met…if not more so.'

'Save your compliments for someone who might appreciate them,' Sara snapped, but she could do nothing about the curl of heat igniting in her stomach, or the telltale tide of red that washed over her cheeks.

'Amazing…you can still blush.'

'I am not blushing, I am angry,' she half-lied. 'After last night I hoped never to see you again. What are you doing here, anyway? Shouldn't you be entertaining your breakfast guests?'

Sara fought to remain calm, but with Guido towering over her, wearing only khaki shorts with a shirt hanging open off his broad shoulders, there was way too much of him on display for her peace of mind. She couldn't help her eyes straying down over his chest, following the light dusting of curling black body hair that encircled small male nipples and arrowed down beneath the waistband of his shorts. And why didn't he pull his damn shorts up? They were almost falling off his lean hips. She could see the hollows of his pelvic bones, for heaven's sake.

'So good of you to be concerned about my manners,' he drawled mockingly. 'But breakfast is over, and while my crew are giving the guests a tour of my yacht I—with the encouragement of your captain—have come looking for you. Dave is worried you might get lost and miss the boat.' Flinging a casual arm across her shoulders, he added, 'I assured him I would find you and escort you back to the harbour. Nice man Dave—very informative.'

She cast a sidelong glance up at Guido. What had Dave told him? she wondered as she tried to shrug off his arm without much luck. He simply tightened his grip on her shoulder and, unwilling to make a scene on the beach, she gritted her teeth and bore the embrace.

'Don't look so worried. Come on—we have time for coffee and a talk before you have to leave.'

The weight of his arm around her shoulders and the warmth of his big body pressed against her side set every nerve end in her body on edge.

'Wait a minute.' Sara dug her heels in the sand. 'I don't want a coffee, and I don't need you to escort me anywhere.' And she certainly did not want to talk to him, reopen old wounds.

'You may not need me to escort you, but after last night you can't pretend you don't want me.' And slipping his other hand around her waist, shopping bag and all, he hauled her against him and kissed her in broad daylight, on a public beach, in front of parents and children. So much for not making a scene. Guido was doing it for her, was her last sensible thought.

Surprised at his audacity, and with the sandals in her hand jammed against her thigh, it should have been embarrassing. But at the first touch of his lips against hers her pulse raced, her temperature soared, and she surrendered without a murmur. Not quite without a murmur. Shamefully she moaned her displeasure when he finally broke the kiss and lifted his dark head to stare down into her dazed blue eyes.

'Shall we start again?' For a second Sara thought he meant their relationship, and fear and fervour in equal parts battled for supremacy in her stunned mind—until he set her free and stepped back.

'Good morning, Sara.' He smiled and made a slight bow. 'It is a pleasure to meet you again.' The teasing smile curving his firm lips was reflected in his eyes, making him look for a moment like the happy-go-lucky sexy young man she had married. 'Can I persuade you to share a cup of coffee with me for old times' sake before you leave?' His dark eyes gleaming, he added, 'Please.'

It was the *please* that convinced her. 'Put like that, how can I refuse?' Sara capitulated. After all, she told herself, what harm could there be in having a farewell cup of coffee with the man? She was leaving in an hour and she would never see him again. It was an amazing coincidence that they had met this time after almost a decade,

CHAPTER FOUR

SEATED at a table beneath a straw umbrella, outside a beach café, Sara let a wry smile curve her lips as Guido, with an arch of an eyebrow in the half-asleep waiter's direction, stirred the man into a bustle of activity. The table was wiped and their order taken. Everyone jumped to Guido's bidding. And years ago she had been no exception.

A single look from his incredible black eyes and she would have lain down and died for him. A particular look and she had lain down *anywhere* with him, to be swept away in a storm of passion, more times than she could count. Until sadly she had been forced to realise passion was not enough. Once it had consumed her and almost destroyed her, but never again…

'You look pensive,' Guido remarked as the

waiter set two coffees down on the table. 'Sorry to be leaving?'

Sara picked up her cup. 'No,' she said coolly, taking a sip of the hot coffee and glancing at him over the top of her cup. 'I will be glad to get home and back to work,' she added, without thinking.

'Ah, yes—work.' His eyes gleamed. 'Dave let me in on your secret this morning. In fact we had quite a talk, and I let him in on ours.'

The cup clattered down on the saucer, spilling coffee all over the place. 'You did what?' Sara demanded, horrified.

'Tut-tut, Sara—you look a little upset.' His dark eyes mocked her. 'I wonder why? According to Dave, you and Pat have been best friends for over six years. You were the bridesmaid at their wedding, and you are not a professional cook but an accountant, and out of the generosity of your soul you cut short your own holiday and agreed to help them out this past week. He waxed quite lyrical about you, so naturally I assumed you must have mentioned that you had been married.'

'You told Dave?' she said slowly.

'Yes.' He shrugged his broad shoulders. 'Dave was surprised, but not half as surprised as Pat. She never knew you had been married. My, oh, my! What a thing to keep hidden from your best friend,' he taunted.

'Oh, no!' Sara cried, appalled. She could just imagine the grilling she would get from Pat…

'Though given the way you behaved, maybe shame kept you quiet.' Guido smiled unpleasantly. 'After all, if your best friends knew you for the money-hungry little vixen you are, I doubt they would be half as happy trusting their accounts to you.'

'Trusting…' she spluttered, and as the full import of his words sank in rage erupted inside her. Her hand shot out in an arc, but before she could make contact with his handsome face her wrist was caught and held by the ruthless strength of his cruel fingers.

'I allowed you one strike last night, but I have no intention of allowing you another,' he said menacingly. 'And if you are wondering what to do next I have a suggestion. Try being less volatile and listen.'

'You can have nothing to say that would interest me in the slightest,' she spat back, her eyes moist with pain and anger. 'And let go of my wrist. You're hurting me.'

'You don't know the meaning of hurting,' he snarled. His dark eyes captured hers, and for a moment she thought she caught a glimpse of bitterness in the black depths. 'Your beautiful feminine façade disguises a devious hard woman that nothing could hurt. You were supposedly so upset over the loss of our baby, but within hours were flinging out wild accusations to all and sundry. You caused havoc in my family. We thought you were confused after the accident, and we tried to help you with the best medical help money could buy. Yet as soon as you were well you took the first opportunity to run back to London with a quarter of a million pounds in your pocket. So don't make me laugh with your crocodile tears.' And he flung her wrist free.

'You dare to say that to me? You bastard.' She was goaded to retaliate at the mention of the baby. 'You pitiful excuse for a man—you make me sick.'

'And here I thought it was your pregnancy that did that,' he drawled mockingly.

'Very funny. Ha-bloody-Ha!' she swore. She knew very well what he was referring to. She had never suffered from morning sickness at the start of her pregnancy, but once they'd moved to Italy she'd begun to feel sick morning and evening. In fact in her darkest hours after losing the baby she had wondered if his hateful cousin Caterina was responsible for that as well. She certainly wouldn't have put it past her. But all that had concerned Guido was the interruption to his sex life.

As for trust—his had been non-existent where she was concerned, and the injustice of it all made the anger and resentment she had harboured for years finally break free. She told him exactly how she felt.

'I was eighteen, you were my husband, and I was stupid enough to believe I could trust you and depend on your loyalty and support. Instead you stuck me in that mausoleum of a house and left me alone and your awful family made my life hell. Your precious cousin Caterina told me *she* was your real love, and she and her mother never stopped telling me you had only married me because I was pregnant. Your father did the same—and much worse. He treated me like dirt beneath his feet, especially after he learned, to quote him directly, that I had "no breeding".'

His dark eyes narrowed derisively on her furious face. 'I was there, Sara, and my family offered you nothing but friendship and respect. Your stories are wasted on me. I know you for the liar you are,' he opined sardonically.

'You do not know me at all,' she flashed back. Sara was on a roll, and his supercilious superiority infuriated her even more. 'And you were never there. You were either on a business trip to Rome or Paris and the like, or you worked sixteen hours a day at the office in Naples. The only time I saw you was in bed, and when I tried to talk to you there you had other things on your mind,' she threw at him scathingly. 'And even when we were in bed the sainted Caterina walked in on us. Apparently accustomed to wandering into your bedroom. The woman was sick with love of you, and you encouraged her.

'As for when I lost our baby—you turned up eight hours after the fact, explaining you'd had to cut short a meeting in Geneva, and patted my head and told me not to worry. I was young and there would be other children. You didn't listen to a word I said about the accident that caused me to miscarry. And I don't care what you and your family want to believe. I *know* what happened, and young Aldo had a pretty good idea as well.'

'*Basta*! You go too far,' Guido roared. 'Caterina is dead—killed in a car accident.'

'Poetic justice,' Sara muttered under her breath, unable to help herself. Thankfully Guido was too incensed to notice.

'And as for Aldo I will not have you bringing a mere boy, as he was at the time, into your delusions.'

'I'm not surprised,' Sara fired back sarcastically 'He must be…what…about twenty-five now? Able to make his views heard. Not that he would bother. He probably knows that an arrogant, conceited swine like you would never accept that your judgment was less than perfect.' She was sick of arguing and sick at heart…

She knew Caterina had pushed her down the steps to the beach. She *knew*, and after her miscarriage she had told Guido as much and demanded he call the police. Both he and his parents had refused, insisting she was confused after the fall. When she had argued her case, they had brought the gardener to her hospital bed to refute her claim. The gardener had sworn *he* had been with Caterina the whole time discussing a new layout for the front garden. He had only discovered Sara unconscious on the beach after Caterina had gone indoors, when he had walked around the house to the rear garden that held a swimming pool and three terraces that led down to the beach.

All the adults, the doctor included, had decided she was confused after being unconscious for over an hour and breaking her arm, and delusional and depressed because of losing her baby.

Sara sighed, and picked up her coffee cup. What was the point in raking over the past? Apparently Caterina was dead, and she could not pretend she was sorry. Only young Aldo had been inclined to believe her story, but at fifteen nobody had listened to his opinion. Draining the cup, she replaced it on the table and stood up.

'Wait.' Guido leapt to his feet and put a restraining hand on her shoulder. Looking down into her incredible deep blue eyes, he saw the resentment, the simmering anger, and something else—a resignation he had never seen before.

'I have not finished with you yet.' Guido was surprised she'd had the nerve to reiterate her ridiculous story and dare to involve his brother. Yet for the first time since she had left him he allowed a doubt to surface. Sara was right about one aspect of their marriage. He had discovered within days of taking over the business after his father's heart attack that the old man had let things slide badly. He had worked long hours and gone on quite a few business trips to repair the damage. It had never occurred to him to wonder what his very young wife did all day, left alone with his family.

'You and I were finished a decade ago,' Sara said coldly.

'Marriage—yes,' Guido swiftly agreed. 'But I have a different proposition for you.'

He wanted Sara back in his bed with a hunger and a need he had not felt in years. Other women satisfied him, but the sensuality of this woman tormented him like no other. Her response last night when he kissed her had been incredibly passionate. And even now he could sense the sexual tension simmering beneath her cool façade. He'd never had any problem persuading his numerous lovers into his bed, and Sara had been no exception. He might have to work a little harder this time, given their past, but without being over-confident he had no doubt the result would be the same.

'We are both a lot older and have no illusions about love and marriage and happy-ever-after, Sara,' Guido offered smoothly.

Sara shot Guido an icy glance. 'You've got that right.' She snorted.

Guido had killed her dream of a home and so-called normal family with the brutality of an executioner at the guillotine. He had single-handedly destroyed her ability ever to trust a man again. After they had parted it had felt like a bereavement—but in a way it had been worse, because not only had she lost someone she loved, she had also been forced to face the fact that the caring, passionate man she had thought she loved had never existed except in her imagination. Her confidence and her self-esteem had reached rock bottom, and she still couldn't imagine ever committing to another relationship. She was through with men for good.

She had sworn to herself she would never as long as she lived allow another man to be in a position of control over her. She would be master of her own destiny. She had kept her vow. After three years working for a multinational accountancy firm in London the vow had been the driving force that had made her jump at Sam Thompson's offer of a partnership, allowing her to become her own boss.

'Good. Then there is nothing to stop us being lovers again, *cara mia.*'

The endearment did not faze Sara this time, because she knew it meant nothing. Coolly she looked up into his dark eyes, but inexplicably her heart swooped in her breast at the sultriness in their black depths.

'An adult affair, with no strings attached, just for a while—until this unexpected resurgence of passion between us dies a natural death,' he continued, the hand at her shoulder stroking around to cup the nape of her neck. His arm slid around her waist to hold her closer to his tall, lithe body. 'You walked out too soon last time, sweetheart. I had not had my fill of you.'

Sara's gaze dropped to his mouth and she saw the harsh carnality of his expression, saw that he was deadly serious. He wanted her with a frightening intensity he made no attempt to hide, and to her shame she was tempted. She knew without looking that her breasts had peaked provocatively against the hardness of his bare chest, and she could do nothing about the sudden increase in her pulse.

'If you had hung around a little longer, Sara, you could have made a hell of a lot more money.'

The mention of money had an immediate cooling effect on Sara's traitorous body. The swine had the gall to admit he would have paid more to get rid of her if she had not gone at the first telling, Yet now he had the nerve to suggest he wanted her back in his bed for *a while*. No strings attached.

What was it Peter had said? She was too good to be part of Guido's harem. Well, maybe not, she thought bitterly. After years of celibacy maybe it was time she gave her body a break and took what was on offer. Used Guido the way he wanted to use her. She was sick of being the victim—the celibate female afraid to allow a man into her life in case he tried to take over.

In fact, she reasoned, Guido was the one man she could take to her bed without having to fear. She didn't trust him, she didn't want anything more from him than his body, and he had stated categorically that was all he wanted from her. Her and a handful of other women, depending on his location in the world at any given time, she thought scathingly. He really was a love rat, with a sophisticated woman in every port.

No… She immediately realised the folly of her wayward thoughts. She could never be his lover again; she had too much pride to be one of his harem. But there was nothing stopping her pretending to play the part. Letting the arrogant bastard know she was no longer the naïve teenager she had once been, but a sexually experienced adult and successful career woman. And if she wasn't *actually* sexually experienced…? An article she had read in her secretary's trashy magazine came to mind…

'You mean you want me as your sex buddy?' she asked, in a conversational tone.

A glint of surprise flashed in Guido's eyes but was quickly masked. 'That is not quite how I would have described the relationship I have in mind, Sara,' he murmured huskily, his dark head bending confidently towards hers.

'I believe in America the term is "booty buddy" or "friends with benefits",' she said coolly, placing a restraining hand on his chest. And she wished she hadn't as her palm tingled at the contact with his warm, tanned flesh.

His jaw dropped in disbelief, then he grinned—a devilish, heart-meltingly sensuous grin—and for a moment he looked like the young man she had fallen in love with. 'Sara, you shock me. I would never have believed you knew such terms. But I accept.' And he kissed her.

'You're taking liberties,' she exploded, when she could get her breath back from the devastating effect of his kiss. 'I was not offering.'

'Yes, you were. It is simply a case of arranging the time and place. Now seems good to me. You can collect your luggage and join me on my yacht.'

'No, I damn well can't,' Sara swore. 'I have a job to do—lunch to make for the guests. Then I am flying back to England once we reach Ibiza. I have a career I love and a living to make. The world does not stop because you say so, you arrogant pig.' Shoving out of his arms, she added, 'And fasten your shirt. You look like a beach bum.' With that she picked up her belongings and stormed off down the beach.

'Okay, so maybe I was a bit hasty,' Guido conceded, catching up with her and matching his long stride to her hurried ones. 'When *can* we get together, sex buddy?'

He was laughing at her, and she wanted to throw something at him—let out the hysteria that was mounting inside her. Instead she stalked angrily on.

'I never asked you to be…whatever,' she said sharply, wondering how the hell she had got herself into this ridiculous conversation.

'Maybe not directly. But you know you want to, and I have a busy schedule, so let's get down to dates. How about you cancel your flight and I'll meet you in Ibiza tonight? I will put my aircraft at your disposal to take you back to England tomorrow evening.'

A private aircraft said it all. He was so far out of her league it didn't bear thinking about. But, determined to keep up the appearance of so-phisticated woman, she lifted her chin. 'Sorry—no,' she said sweetly. 'I am off the pill at the moment, and going on past experience I wouldn't trust you and only a condom within touching distance of me.' She laughed lightly. 'We both know that would be a disaster.'

'You're right, of course.' His arm slipped ap-parently casually around her waist as they ap-proached the berthed yachts. 'This weekend is a no-no, and I have to be back in Italy by

Monday. Aldo runs the Italian office, but he married recently and is taking a month off for his honeymoon.'

'Aldo got married?' Sara asked, diverted for a moment from her anger at the man.

'Yes, three days ago—the silly idiot. I tried to warn him he is far too young, but he ignored me.'

Sara glanced up at his scowling face with a warm, reminiscent smile on hers. 'Did he marry Marta?'

'Yes.' Guido's dark eyes narrowed. 'But how did you know about her?' His frown deepened.

'Aldo introduced me. They were the only two people who treated me as a friend when I was in Italy—probably because I was nearer their age than anybody else's,' she said bluntly. 'Give them my congratulations when you see them again. They are a lovely couple.'

'Okay,' Guido agreed. Though he was surprised and slightly uncomfortable at her revelation, it was not something he wanted to pursue now, as they approached the yacht. Time was running out, and he had a more pressing need on his mind. 'But to get back to us.' Stopping beside the gangway, he turned her into his arms. 'I take your point about the pill,' he said, his tone briskly efficient, as if he were addressing a board meeting. 'You take care of that, and I will see you in a month.'

'What—?' Sara opened her mouth to object and Guido took full advantage, kissing her with a hard, hungry passion that took her objection plus her breath away and made her weak at the knees.

Suddenly he set her free, and she half fell against his body. His dark eyes gleamed wickedly down into hers. 'Still as eager as ever to fall into my arms? But we haven't time and we have an audience.' He grinned. 'Don't forget—do the necessary and I'll meet you in London four weeks from today.'

His arrogant conceit amazed her, and it was several seconds before she could bring herself to reply. 'I don't—'

'Come on, Sara.' Dave's voice cut in on her denial that she would agree to any such arrangement. 'We're about to cast off.'

Then the two men were shaking hands like old friends, and Sara was ushered up the gangway by Dave. She glanced over her shoulder to see Guido, a broad grin on his handsome face, lift a hand with four fingers extended before turning towards his own yacht.

'If you wash that bench one more time, it will melt. For heaven's sake, Sara, the galley is immaculate—everything is battened down. Now it's time for you to sit down and talk,' Pat demanded from where she was sitting on the bench beneath the porthole. 'As your best friend, you owe me that much. I can't believe you never mentioned you had been married. And, worse, I can't believe you were dumb enough to let such a marvellous hunk of masculinity—a *rich* hunk at that—get away from you. Were you out of your mind?' She chuckled.

With a reluctant sigh Sara tossed the cloth in the garbage and joined Pat on the bench. 'Not quite,' she said with a wry smile. 'And actually there is nothing much to tell. I met Guido my first year at university. He was a mature student. We met. We had sex. I got pregnant. We got married, and when I miscarried we got a divorce. It was a big mistake all round. Satisfied?'

'Oh, poor you,' Pat murmured, rubbing her stomach. 'I can't imagine losing my baby. It must have been devastating for you, Sara. But why did you never tell me?'

'There didn't seem much point. I met him, married and divorced him within a year. When you came to share my flat three years later I had put the whole unfortunate episode out of my mind. It was just sheer bad luck I had to bump into Guido yesterday after almost a decade.' And, rising to her feet, she added, 'With a bit of good luck I will never see him again in this life.'

'I'm sorry you feel that way,' Pat said tentatively. 'Because Dave and I liked him. In fact Guido has suggested chartering our ship for twelve months when our present bookings are finished, at an extremely generous fee.'

'Guido? Charter this?' Sara exclaimed, waving her hand around the galley. 'What on earth for? He has a flaming great yacht of his own.'

'Apparently he thinks it will be perfect for a charity he supports in Italy for underprivileged boys. A chance to teach them how to sail, and at the same time build their confidence.'

'You must be joking! Guido Barberi hasn't a charitable bone in his body. He is the most arrogant, self-centred man I have ever met.' Recognising the expression on her friend's face, Sara saw she wasn't kidding. 'It's probably a tax break,' she concluded dryly.

She could not imagine Guido wasting his time with children. He certainly hadn't been very upset when she'd miscarried. More relieved, she thought bitterly. He had not even bothered to tell her he wanted her gone; he had taken off to America and let his father do it for him…

'Tax break or not,' Pat said, rising stiffly to her feet, 'given my pregnant state the offer could not have come at a better time. The money will be an absolute lifesaver for Dave and I.'

'Oh, I'm sorry.' Sara slipped an arm around her friend. 'Take no notice of me. Of course it's a great idea, and I'm really pleased for you both. It certainly takes the pressure off you, and now there'll be no rush for you to leave England after you have the baby,' she said, and forced a bright smile to her lips.

'No rush at all.'

And for the next ten minutes Sara listened as Pat talked enthusiastically of the relative benefits of various areas of Greater London, and the best maternity hospitals, and where to rent a home…

CHAPTER FIVE

THREE nights later Sara wandered around the living room of her apartment, unable to settle. She had thought her first day back at work would cure the restlessness she had felt since her Mediterranean cruise. Sam had welcomed her with open arms, said, 'Thank heaven you're back. I'd forgotten how hard it was to work two weeks solid. By the way, you have an appointment in ten minutes with Fred from the Dog and Duck,' and promptly taken himself off to play golf.

From then on Sara had worked hard all day. On returning home she had changed, eaten, washed up, and was now aimlessly wandering around, straightening ornaments like an idiot.

The ringing of her cellphone was a welcome relief and, picking it up from where she had discarded it on the coffee table, she sank down into an armchair and answered.

'Hello—Sara here.'

'This is your knight errant speaking.'

She laughed, and for the next five minutes verbally sparred with the irrepressible Peter Wells, finally agreeing to meet him on Friday evening for dinner.

Closing the phone, she leapt to her feet, feeling much better. It was a lovely summer evening. A brisk walk along the waterfront would do her the world of good, and so, picking up her bag, she placed her phone in the pocket provided and headed for the door. She had only taken two steps when the phone rang again.

'What now, Peter?' She chuckled, assuming it was him.

'Not Peter, but Guido—your ex-husband, remember?' a deep voice drawled mockingly.

'I'm trying very hard to forget—and how did you get my number?' Sara demanded. She certainly had not given it to him.

'Pat was very obliging, and she was sure you

wouldn't mind—not when I told her we had a date arranged. Have you seen a doctor yet?'

'A date... A doctor... What on earth are you talking about? No—don't bother to explain, and don't call me again,' she said furiously.

'Okay—but don't forget it is twenty-six days and counting.' And he had the cheek to laugh.

'You...you...you...' Sara spluttered 'Oh, go boil your head.' And she cut him off.

Her improved mood had been destroyed in moments by the sound of Guido's voice. As for Pat—she would kill her when she saw her again. Striding out of the apartment, she slammed the door behind her.

But it was not so easy to slam the door on her thoughts, or to still the sudden racing of her pulse. She knew Guido could only be teasing—having some fun at her expense—but *why*, after all this time? And why was she letting him bother her? She was never going to see him again. The answer was that simple...

She walked down to the waterfront to where a replica of the old sailing ship the *Cutty Sark* held pride of place. Sitting down on a convenient bench, she stared out over the River Thames. Life went on whatever... The sinking sun gleamed golden red on the smoothly flowing waters as it had done for thousands of years. She glanced back at the old ship and thought of the hundreds of men who must have sailed in the original centuries ago, transporting tea and spices from the Far East and now long gone—a mere speck in the annals of history. It was a sobering thought.

Was she really content to go on denying the sensual part of her nature as she had done for years? Before it had been easy. But the events of last week had shocked her body out of cold storage. Peter's kiss had started the thaw, and Guido's presence had accelerated the process.

Was it because of Peter? A week of his amusing friendship, and for the first time in years she had allowed herself to relax with a man. And then there had been his kiss. Or was it Guido reappearing in her life? But either way she could not sleep at night, her body hot and aching for what it had been denied far too long.

Maybe she *should* see a doctor and get the birth control pill.

She was meeting Peter on Friday. She liked him, enjoyed his company, and after that kiss she knew it would be no hardship to sleep with him.

Not straight away, of course, but eventually...

As for Guido Barberi, he was the past and that was where he would stay. That was it, Sara decided, rising swiftly to her feet. Her mind was made up. She was going to move on, embrace the future, hopefully in the arms of a fit handsome blond Adonis—Peter...

Men had been dating younger women for years, and the twenty-first century was one of equal opportunity so it was perfectly okay for her to date a younger man.

On Friday evening, when she met Peter Wells for dinner, she began to realise the answer was not that simple...

The next morning Sara woke from a deep sleep to the ringing of her telephone.

'Oh, God!' she groaned. She had drunk too much last night, and who could blame her? she thought ruefully. Peter had taken her to a top London fish restaurant, and they had dined on caviar and lobster washed down with the finest champagne. But it had not turned out to be a celebration of their first date and the deeper relationship she had been considering, but a celebration of Peter's new job.

He was flying to Hong Kong today, to take up a promotion as head of his company's Far Eastern office. A job that paid him twice as much as his present position with virtually limitless bonus opportunities. Apparently his boss had offered him the promotion quite out of the blue and he had jumped at the offer.

'Oh, hell.' She groaned again at the insistent ringing of the phone, and, dragging herself up, she picked the phone off the bedside table. 'Yes—yes... Who is it?' Her mouth felt like sandpaper, her head like lead, and a swift glance at the bedroom clock told her it was only seven a.m.

'You sound rough. Had a heavy night, Sara?'

'Guido. I don't believe it,' she muttered darkly. Hangover notwithstanding, her foolish heart still leapt at the instantly recognisable sound of his voice. And the obvious amusement in his tone did not help her temper one bit. 'How I spent my night and with whom is no business of yours,' she snapped.

'Are you alone now?' he demanded, no longer sounding amused.

Let him wonder, Sara thought. She had wondered about him and other women, especially Caterina, for most of their brief marriage. The fact that the woman was now dead did not change anything. She ignored his question.

'What the hell are you calling for at this ungodly hour? Or at all,' she demanded.

'Simply to remind you, sweetheart, that it is three weeks and counting.'

There was a confidence in his tone that infuriated her. Pursuing women was a lifelong amusement for Guido; it was just her bad luck that seeing her again had tweaked his interest. But she wasn't going to get into an argument with him. He would never change, and by next week someone else would have captured his interest.

'Go take a hike, Guido.' She heard him chuckle.

'Ah, Sara, obviously you are softening

towards me. Taking a hike is so much better than boiling my head.'

His total conceit and his perverse humour was the last straw for Sara. 'Guido. I would have to be soft in the head to ever see you again. It is not going to happen—not in three weeks' time, not in three million years' time. I trust that is clear enough for you? Don't call me again.'

She slammed the phone down, and when it rang again she checked the caller ID and ignored it. Later, when she was out shopping for the weekend, she bought a new cellphone and, despite the huge inconvenience, dumped the old.

Guido, a deep frown creasing his broad brow, opened the French doors in the dark-panelled breakfast room and walked out into the garden. Sara had been right about one thing. With his father an invalid and Aldo away he had spent the last week working from home—probably the longest he had actually spent in the place since he was a teenager—and the place *was* like a mausoleum.

His dark, brooding gaze skimmed over the

swimming pool and followed the line of terraces to where the steps led down to the beach. The steps where he had effectively lost his wife and his unborn child. For years he had dismissed the whole affair from his mind, but seeing Sara again had brought everything back.

Especially the erotic memories. Her gorgeous body entwined with his, her silken skin, the cute dimples, her perfect breasts with the exquisitely responsive rosy peaks he had suckled so many times. And he was determined to do so again…

A grim smile curved his hard mouth. It wasn't just lust or simple frustration because he had gone five weeks without a woman.

No—it was retribution time…

She was running scared. She had slammed the phone down on him for a second time, refused his next call and now changed her phone number. No woman had refused Guido in years—if ever. Usually he was fighting them off, and Sara's reluctance was a new experience for him. An experience he rather liked, in a weird way. His sex life had become pretty predictable for the last few years—and, if he was honest, a little boring. He was a man who loved a challenge in business and in life, and Sara provided a challenge he would enjoy overcoming.

Without conceit he knew he was a good lover. He also knew that he only had to get her in his arms again and she would be his. The chestnut-haired, blue-eyed beauty he had kissed and caressed ten days ago was no way immune to him, and she knew it. An image of her dress hanging open, her near naked body his for the taking, filled his mind, and involuntarily he ran his hand along his jaw. His until he had made that stupid comment and she had punched him...

A wry smile twisted his firm lips. Sara could not help herself. She had a fiery temperament in bed and out. He needed to change his approach. No more trying to coax her into his arms with teasing calls. No—the next time they met she would have no warning and no escape.

Sara was going to be his again for as long as it suited him...

Sara set out for her office in good spirits, her high-heeled sandals tapping out a joyful rhythm on the pavement and accentuating the sway of her hips beneath the blue straight-skirted dress she was wearing. The short-sleeved shirt-styled bodice revealed a tempting glimpse of cleavage, and the wide matching belt made her waist look incredibly small. Her gleaming hair was swept up in a loose chignon. August had arrived, the sun was shining, and it was over four weeks since she had left Majorca and Guido.

Although she had changed her mobile number and had no contact with him, for some reason she had still felt vaguely threatened. But with the weekend of their so-called date come and gone, she felt as if a weight had lifted off her shoulders.

'Good morning, everyone.' She breezed into the office and greeted Tim, the junior accountant, her secretary, Jan, and the other office staff with a broad smile on her face. 'Beautiful day.'

'Someone is in a good mood.' Jan grinned. 'And I am about to make your day even better. How does lunch sound?' She mentioned the name of a luxury hotel in the middle of London.

Sara paused on the way to her own office. 'Great, but not very likely—unless we have won the Lotto and nobody told me,' she quipped. All the staff had formed a syndicate ages ago, and so far they had won a grand total of ten pounds.

'I wish,' Jan shot back. 'But no such luck—though if the prospective client Mr Thompson has arranged for you to have lunch with today signs on the dotted line our Christmas bonuses could be a lot better this year.'

'Sam has arranged for me to take a client to lunch at a five-star luxury hotel?' Sara queried in amazement. 'Wait a minute; we *are* talking about the one overlooking the Embankment? In the centre of London?' She emphasised the location. 'And not some pub that I'm not aware of?'

Sara knew her elderly partner well, and he was a bit tight-fisted. But in between playing golf and drinking at the nineteenth hole, or in his local pub, he did occasionally pick up new clients to add to the very healthy list of those he had had for years.

Occasionally he actually put in a full day at the office...

'I kid you not. But needless to say Sam is not paying for it. You are to be the guest,' Jan responded. 'Sam rang just before you arrived. He met a Mr Billy Johnson at the weekend, who apparently has been thinking of changing his accountant. The accountant he has used for years is nearing retirement, and he wants someone younger, someone up to date with modern taxation law, European directives and the like. Well, of course that cuts out Sam—but, never one to miss a trick, Sam sold the man on you. Apparently Mr Johnson already has a lunch date arranged at the hotel today, with his financial partner, and he suggested you join them. Of course Sam agreed on your behalf, and he also said to tell you to make a point of mentioning you worked for one of the top four International accountancy firms in the world before joining this firm. Convince the man we are a highly professional and thoroughly modern well-established business, renowned for our discreet and personal service, and of course we can save the guy a fortune…'

'Exactly what kind of business are we talking about here?' Sara queried dryly. 'Knowing Sam it could be anything.' She was still smarting from the last client he had put her way. A rather shady bookmaker who also owned a string of racing greyhounds. Sam had met him in the Dog and Duck, the owner of which was also one of their clients.

Jan laughed. 'I've checked out Mr Johnson. He owns a fleet of pleasure boats on the Thames.'

'I might have guessed. One of his boats probably docked here once. I've never heard of him before—here's hoping Sam didn't meet this one in the pub.'

'Hopefully not,' Jan responded. 'But it sounds like a promising account.'

Sara chuckled. 'Yes, you're probably right. According to an article I read recently there are now more pleasure boats ferrying people up and down the Thames than there have been since the nineteenth century. Apart from the building of the London Eye and the Dome, and all the tourists wanting to visit the Greenwich Observatory increasing the traffic, a lot of local people travel by boat into the city centre instead of on the train. In fact I think I'll take one up to London. I can get off at Embankment, and it's a short walk from there to the hotel.'

* * *

Later Sara wondered ruefully if it had been such a good idea as she stepped off the ferry and onto the landing stage at Embankment. It was a quarter to twelve, her hair was blown all over the place, and the spray from some idiot in a power boat had splashed all over her. Once on dry land she tried to redo her hair. But, having lost a couple of pins, she had no choice but to leave it loose. She repaired her lipstick and prayed the damp patches on her businesslike shirt-styled dress would dry out while she walked briskly towards the hotel.

Guido watched Sara enter the hotel from the discreet position he had taken in one corner of the foyer. He saw her smile at the receptionist as she asked for the restaurant, and a shaft of pure sensation shot through him, hot and hard. His mouth tightened into a grim line of control and his dark eyes narrowed as he watched her walk towards the restaurant—as did every man in the vicinity, he noted sardonically.

And why not? She was beautiful, statuesque, curvy and full-lipped, with golden brown hair.

She looked totally natural. The years since they had first met had given her poise. She had that indefinable something called style. There was none of the heavily made-up plastic look that so many otherwise beautiful women seemed to favour. She was simply stunning, with an underlying sexuality that any red-blooded male could not fail to recognize, and his body hardened further at his wayward thoughts. No way was he going to lunch with her in this state. He wanted her alone and amenable for what he had in mind.

A few minutes later Billy Johnson entered the hotel. Guido greeted him, and with an apologetic smile informed him that he had to wait for an important conference call. He told him to start lunch without him.

If he didn't make it in time he suggested Billy and their guest join him in his suite later. But Billy was not to spoil the surprise by revealing Guido's name.

Sara made it to the restaurant at five to twelve. The *maître d'* guided her to an empty table set for three, and suggested she might like an aperitif while she waited for her host. Sara refused, instead pouring herself a glass of water and taking a sip before casually glancing around. She felt rather conspicuous on her own, and heaved a sigh of relief when a few minutes later the *maître d'* reappeared with a short, rather attractive and slightly plump man at his side, thirty-something, with greying hair and a moustache. For a second Sara thought he looked vaguely familiar, but dismissed the notion when he began to talk.

Mr Johnson was a genuine Londoner and a delight, Sara decided half an hour later, having eaten a delicious seafood starter and drunk a glass of wine. Billy, as he'd insisted she call him, had apologised for the absence of his financial partner. Apparently he was expecting a conference call and had insisted they continue without him.

Sara had given Billy a résumé of her career to date, and he had seemed very impressed. Then he had enthusiastically outlined his business, and explained his expansion plans.

With rumours circulating in the press that the

new owners of the Millennium Dome were odds-on favourites to get the licence for the first super casino in Britain, it was an opportune time to add to his fleet of riverboats. He envisaged a sched-uled service to the casino, plus a couple of bigger deluxe boats with on-board restaurants that would provide a dining experience on the Thames before hitting the gaming tables. He was also hoping to extend his fleet of barges, as more and more freight was being transported on the river.

Sara grinned as she put her cutlery down on the table, having eaten the best fillet steak she had ever tasted.

'That was superb, Billy, and I think your ideas for expanding are fantastic. I can assure you that if you give Thompson & Beecham your business you will not be disappointed. I know I could manage your accounts for you efficiently and imaginatively—but within the law, of course.'

'I agree,' he said, and glanced at his watch. 'But I really would like you to meet my partner before signing on the dotted line, so to speak. He is staying here, but I guess his call is taking longer than he expected. If you have time I could take you to meet him. I'm sure he can't be tied up much longer.'

Relaxed by good food, good wine and the prospect of a great new client, Sara agreed.

A short ride in the elevator and Billy rapped on the door of his partner's room. The door opened and Billy stepped back to let her go first—the perfect gentleman.

Smiling, Sara walked straight into the room and turned to the man who was standing back from the opened the door. Something like an electric shock went through her. It was Guido, and the shock had nothing to do with his unexpected presence and everything to do with the sudden leap of her pulse and the surge of heat that embarrassingly stained her cheeks.

He was wearing a perfectly tailored pale grey suit, a crisp shirt and silk tie—the epitome of the successful tycoon—and he was looking at her with a cynical smile on his handsome face and a gleam of triumph in his night-black eyes. Then he spoke...

'We meet again, Sara.'

Ignoring him, she turned swiftly to Billy

Johnson in time to see him close the door behind them.

'This is your partner?' she demanded.

'Yes, Sara.' She saw the slightly wary look in his eyes. 'I didn't mention his name before because Guido wanted to surprise you. But you seem more angry than surprised.'

'Anger does not begin to explain how I feel at this moment,' she shot back. 'Do you actually *have* a business?'

'Yes, of course.' He looked puzzled. 'You don't remember me, do you? I was a witness at your wedding, and Guido helped me out later, when my father died and I took over the business. Everything I told you is true. I *do* want you to be my firm's accountant and I assumed this would be a romantic reunion.'

So that was why she had thought he looked vaguely familiar. Not that she had noticed anything much on her wedding day. She'd only had eyes for Guido...

'Romantic— We are divorced.' Sara shook her head in disgust and glanced around the elegant room, seeing it was a sitting room. This must be a suite. What else but the best for Guido? Finally she turned and looked up into Guido's darkly handsome face, her brilliant blue eyes clashing with his.

'I suppose this is your idea of a joke?'

His dark eyes narrowed slightly. 'No joke, Sara. I am quite serious in backing Billy's expansion plans, and his intention to employ Thompson & Beecham as his company accountant. You're a professional woman—surely you don't have a problem with that?' he queried smoothly.

Sara was proud of what she had achieved in her career, and she did not appreciate having a mega-rich swine like Guido taking a dig at her professionalism. But she wasn't stupid. She knew she had been set up.

Billy cut in. 'He's right, Sara. I like you, and I know we will get along fine businesswise. As for Guido—he is really only a sleeping partner.'

But who with? Sara wondered, her blue eyes flashing to where Guido stood. His handsome face was bland, but she saw the amused quirk of his lips and suddenly she felt threatened.

'Look—I have to dash.' Billy spoke into the

lengthening silence. 'You and Guido talk it over and I'll give you a call tomorrow, Sara. We can set up a meeting.' Two seconds later Billy was out of the door.

CHAPTER SIX

SARA turned to follow him, but a large hand curved around her arm and held her back. She spun around and looked belligerently at Guido.

'Well? What is this all about, Guido? And don't insult my intelligence by pretending you did not put Billy Johnson up to this. Even if the man is genuine and does want a new accountant I bet our small firm was not top of his list.'

Guido smiled. The predatory smile of a wolf scenting its prey. His hand on her bare arm moved slightly, his thumb stroking the inner curve of her elbow to devastating effect. Her stomach curled, and as his dark gaze roamed insolently over her she could feel herself flushing.

'Oh, I think you know.' His black eyes returned to her face. 'You're not a naïve teenager any more, Sara. I think you know very well.'

And for a long moment he held her gaze, telling her without words exactly what he wanted. She would have had to be lacking all five of her senses not to realise business was the last thing on his mind…

Sara felt a shiver of fear go through her. It had to be fear. The alternative was too shaming to accept.

'No—no, I don't,' she lied, and took a step back. But Guido followed, his hand still firmly around her arm. 'None of this makes any sense.' She shook her head. 'Why would a mega-rich guy like you bother to finance Billy Johnson?'

He shrugged. 'Billy and I were on the same course at university. Like me, he wanted to expand his financial knowledge before joining his father in their boat business. He had already completed a five-year apprenticeship under his father's tutelage to be a Waterman, and had got a licence to drive a tug or passenger vessel between Teddington Lock and the North Sea. He is now a member of the Worshipful Company of Waterman and Lighterman—a system that has been in place for over five hundred years. Apparently your Queen still entrusts them with the task of transporting the Crown Jewels to and from parliament whenever she opens it. It is quite a fascinating business, and in the same field as mine: transport. So naturally we kept in touch, and I helped him out when he needed it.'

Sara heard the enthusiasm in his voice, but she was still surprised that he had bothered with such a relatively small enterprise. But then again he probably made money out of the deal, she thought cynically. 'Good for you. But why this elaborate charade to get me here? You could have just called.'

He raised an eyebrow. 'You put the phone down on me, remember? Not once but twice. And then you changed your number.' For an instant she saw a flare of raw anger in Guido's eyes, then it was gone. In its place was a cool, slightly arrogant regard.

Sara was nowhere near as cool, and her cheeks turned a guilty shade of pink. Why, she had no idea. 'Yes, well—it seems you had no trouble finding out where I work. You could have called me there.'

'The thought did occur to me—but why give you the chance to slam the phone down on me again?' he offered dryly. 'I know you too well, Sara. You're hopelessly impulsive, and you have the outraged female act down to perfection.'

'I am not. I do not,' she denied, incensed by his comment and hanging on to her cool by a thread.

His dark eyes narrowed mockingly on her flushed defiant face. 'You lunched alone with a man you thought you were meeting for the first time. You are in a man's suite—a man whose name you did not even know when you walked in the door. Now, I would call that impulsive— if not downright foolish,' he drawled mockingly.

His hand left her arm to rest on the wall beside her head, and instinctively she moved back until she felt the door panels press against her spine. Her stomach muscles clenched into a knot of tension as she stared warily up at him.

'But, hey! I'm not complaining, Sara. Impulsiveness in a sex buddy could be a good trait.' His deep voice dropped to a husky drawl that quivered along her nerve endings as he added, 'Though I will bow to your superior knowledge of the subject.'

He smiled, a slow curve of his sensuous mouth, and dark eyes lit with wicked amusement held hers. 'Personally I have never thought of the women in my life in quite that way before, but I like the idea.'

Cynically Sara noted the plural. But she could feel the heat of his great body reaching out to her, smell the tantalising scent of his aftershave. He wasn't even touching her but she felt her breath quicken. She knew he was just teasing her, much the same as he had done in the past. Then it had been about her innocence, which he had found beguiling, but now it was about her so-called sexual experience. Yet in a weak moment she found she rather liked the idea as well...

Until suddenly she realised what she was inviting...

'Well, I don't,' she said tersely, and raised a restraining hand to rest on his shirtfront He was too close and too personal, and she had to be mad to be standing here...

'Are you sure about that, Sara?' He placed his free hand on the wall at the other side of her, effectively trapping her. 'Or is it just female pique? Maybe you're angry because I missed our date on Saturday?' he offered facetiously. 'If so, accept my apology. I got tied up.'

'We didn't have a date. It was a joke,' she said, her voice terse. 'And you damn well know it. A joke that is wearing very thin—so just drop it.' She could feel the rise and fall of his chest against her palm, feel the lightest brush of his thighs against her as he inched closer still.

'So you didn't get the pill?' he prompted softly, his breath caressing her cheek

Between trying to fight the blush that threatened and sinking back into the solid door, away from Guido's towering frame, Sara was between a rock and hard place. Was he mocking? Did he expect an answer?

And what was she thinking of letting the man intimidate her again—something she'd sworn she would never do? Where was her backbone?

'As it happens, yes—I did.' She saw the flash of surprise in his black eyes and it encouraged her to expand. 'For Peter's benefit.' She was not going to let Guido think she had turned into some sad sexless woman after she'd left him.

For a long moment he simply looked at her, and bravely she held his gaze. The air between them was fraught with tension, and something in the depths of his black eyes made her pulse race and her temperature rise. She licked her suddenly dry lips and swallowed hard.

Then he spoke.

'Pity for you Wells is now halfway around the world in Hong Kong… But we'd better get down to business. I'm a busy man—after all, that is why you are here.' And, spinning on his heel, he strolled across to a desk and picked up the house telephone. He turned back to face her. 'Would you like coffee? Or something stronger?'

Stunned by his abrupt withdrawal, it took a second or two for Sara to focus. When she did, she knew this was her chance to run…to leave and never look back. And also, she acknowledged, to look like a frightened and unsophisticated fool… Whereas Guido looked incredibly smooth and businesslike, leaning against the table with a slightly mocking gleam in his dark eyes. He *expected* her to run. Well, she damn well wasn't giving him the satisfaction…

A memory from the past flashed in her mind. Guido as a student had always been casually dressed. When they'd moved in together and she had discovered he had two suits in the wardrobe—one dark and one light—she had stupidly suggested one was for funerals and the other for weddings. He had looked at her oddly, but agreed.

He had worn the light one on their wedding day, and that was the only time she had ever seen him in a suit until they'd moved to Italy. Then he'd worn nothing but suits, and she had barely recognised the happy, teasing student she had married beneath the aggressive business person he'd morphed into.

But then she had never really known Guido at all… With the benefit of hindsight she realised his year in England had probably been the equivalent of the gap years students took today. He certainly hadn't needed to go travelling, given all the places he had told her he had already visited. His year out had been a brief re-bellion against settling down in the family business, and unfortunately she had got caught up in the venture.

'If it takes you so long to choose a drink, it doesn't say much for your decision-making in business, Sara,' he drawled sardonically.

'Coffee, please,' she said in a clipped voice, straightening her shoulders and crossing to where two sofas framed an occasional table. She sank gracefully down on to one. She could be the consummate professional when she had to be, and if he wanted to play this farce out to the bitter end she was not going to be the one to back down…

The coffee was ordered and arrived. Guido lounged back on the opposite sofa, firing ques-tions at her about her qualifications, her work ex-perience and Thompson & Beecham in general.

It was surreal, Sara thought, drinking coffee and coolly answering her ex-husband's questions.

When he said, 'Right, I agree with Billy—the account is yours,' Sara picked up her bag and rose to her feet.

'Well, in that case I will say thank you and leave.' She had no intention of taking Billy Johnson on as a client. She would think of something to tell Sam, but she certainly wasn't telling Guido. She didn't trust him an inch, and the way he made her feel she didn't trust herself around him.

'Very polite. Is that it?' he asked, his dark eyes lifting to clash with hers. 'Not a very enthusiastic acceptance of what will be a very lucrative deal for your firm,' he drawled mockingly.

She just had to grit her teeth, be pleasant and get out of here, Sara told herself firmly. 'Yes, well…I am not the gushing type, but I am of course delighted to do business with you.' The lie almost choked her. 'But now I really must leave…'

Guido's eyes narrowed sardonically on her beautiful face. He knew she was lying and trying not to show it, but that was no surprise. She had lied to him in the past. The difference was that now he could see the lies coming, and it didn't bother him. He was not interested in her character or lack of it, but in her body.

Slowly he rose to his feet. Anticipation was

part of the pleasure in bedding a woman, but he was growing tired of the game.

'If you say so,' he agreed with a reciprocal smile, fully aware that *her* smile had never reached her eyes and that her patience was strained to the limit. 'If you have to leave now, allow me to escort you to the street and get you a cab.' He placed a hand lightly at her waist to guide her and felt her tense. She was definitely not immune to him.

'Shame we didn't have much time to talk.' He let his gaze drop down to linger on the shadowed curve of her cleavage for a moment, before returning it to her face and taking a step in the direction of the door.

'Some other time, perhaps,' she murmured, and he hid a grin at the obvious relief in her startlingly blue eyes as the prospect of escape drew nearer.

'Yes, of course,' he agreed. 'I was talking to Pat and Dave last week,' he continued conversationally. 'They told me they hadn't spoken to you for a while, and they have so much news. I don't suppose they'll mind if I tell you. They will probably be in London by the end of the month—they have already found an apartment to rent—via the internet, apparently—and Pat's already checking out hospitals for the birth. I have agreed to charter their yacht in two weeks' time for a year. We only have the contract to sign and the fee to be paid, and they are delighted at the prospect of spending a year here. That's providing nothing goes wrong, of course...'

Guido waited for her reaction, and knew his words had hit home when she stopped dead—as he had intended them to.

As the import of his supposedly friendly conversation registered in Sara's mind she stopped. From congratulating herself on a lucky escape, she was now filled with a sense of dread. She tilted her chin to stare up into Guido's black, expressionless eyes. In that moment she was reminded of another time and another place, and his father with just that hard look on his face. Suddenly everything made a horrible kind of sense.

She must have been blind not to see it coming. Her partner Sam Thompson, tempted with a lucrative new account for their business. And now the subtle suggestion that the deal Guido had made with her two best friends might fall through. The deal Sara knew Pat and Dave needed quite desperately.

'What could possibly go wrong?' she asked in a tight voice.

'In business, Sara, anything can happen.' He shrugged his broad shoulders. 'Circumstances change…people get a better offer. Or—as you should know better than most—' there was a note in his voice that sent a shiver down her spine '—they simply change their mind.'

Sara's mind raced. She knew he was taunting her, and she knew she should rise above his thinly veiled threat and walk away. But her temper got the better of her.

'You pig, Guido,' she spat, and her blue eyes clashed with his, flashing fire. 'You really expect me to sleep with you to save my friends?'

'I didn't say that,' Guido mocked and, looping an arm around her waist, drew her inexorably closer to his tall frame. 'I am shocked you have such a poor impression of me, Sara.'

The fiend was baiting her, and she burned to lash out at him, but the thought of Pat stopped her.

'But whatever you want to believe is fine with me,' he added tauntingly and, lifting one long finger, he traced the line of her jaw down her throat, lacing his fingers in the silken strands of hair trailing over one shoulder to tug it back and tilt her face up to his.

Sara swallowed hard and felt the blood flow thicker through her veins. She saw the sensual knowledge in his dark, heavy-lidded eyes, heard it in his deep, husky voice.

'So long as you end up in my bed,' he prompted silkily, and bent his handsome head. 'Which you and I both know is where you want to be.'

His supreme masculine confidence and his thinly disguised attempt to blackmail her into his bed disgusted her. But the warmth of his breath caressing her cheek and the devastating sensuality in his night-black eyes made her traitorous body react with the old helpless longing.

Sara briefly closed her eyes, trying to fight the fatal attraction Guido held for her. Now was the moment to leave, she told herself.

But his arm around her waist held her pressed to his hard body, and he was tugging her head back still further. His sensuous mouth brushed hers and she shivered. She tried to resist, but his firm lips and tongue stroking seductively against hers was too much of a temptation, and helplessly her lips parted, giving him access.

Welcoming him with an instinctively provocative slide of her tongue, she felt the shivers turn to shudders of sensuous delight she could not control. When he lifted his head and stared into her glittering blue eyes she could not look away.

'You know you want to,' Guido drawled huskily, his slumberous gaze dropping to her softly parted lips. And then his mouth was on hers again, her hands reached for his broad shoulders, and the moment was lost…

She felt his long fingers stroke through her hair and down to her breast, gasped for air when his mouth left hers and groaned when his lips skimmed her cheek to nuzzle her ear. The warmth of his breath and the husky Italian words he murmured resonated though every nerve in her body and her body reacted with bone-melting enthusiasm. Her legs felt weak, and she was barely aware when his fingers deftly opened the buttons of her dress to slip beneath the scrap of lace covering her breast. The second his nails raked a burgeoning peak heat surged like wildfire through her veins. She heard low guttural moans and knew she was the culprit. But she had not the will to stop them. She did not even try…

She felt the nip of his teeth on one small earlobe and then his mouth found hers again. Like a starving child, she was so hungry for him she kissed him back with a mindless passion, a need that overwhelmed her completely. She could not get enough of the sleek softness of his mouth, the skilful thrust of his tongue, the exquisite sensations of his fingers on her breast tugging on an engorged nipple. She pressed closer, her fingers raking through his hair, and felt the rigid length of his erection against her belly, the increasing moisture between her thighs. She writhed against him.

'Steady,' Guido husked, lifting his head and

lifting her up into his arms. 'We are wearing too many clothes and the bed is next door.'

Wild-eyed, Sara stared at him, too dazed to speak. When he lowered her to her feet in the bedroom she swayed a little, still staring, but now with greedy fascination. Guido removed his tie, his suit and shirt, his socks—the lot—with the minimum of effort, and stood before her totally naked.

Before she had always thought he was gorgeous, with a wonderful body—the perfect man. Sara sucked in a shuddering breath. Now he was physically magnificent. His shoulders were slightly broader than she remembered, his chest and stomach muscles more clearly defined, and in his aroused state he was the most erotically virile male it was possible to imagine.

'You never used to be so slow, Sara.' He smiled a wide, heart-stopping smile and reached for her, then deftly removed every scrap of her clothing and stepped back.

She had no sense of shame…no sense at all… His dark molten eyes washed over her and it was like a caress. The heat in her blood flamed higher.

'*Dio*, you are exquisite,' he breathed and, resting his hands on her waist, he simply stared. Then he stroked his hand slowly up over her breast, rolling the aching peak between his finger and thumb. A low groan escaped her.

'You like that…you always did.' He chuckled and lifted his hands to her throat, threading his fingers through her hair to hold her face up to his. 'You want this, Sara?' he asked, his voice low and sensuous.

Want was too tame a word. She was desperate… 'Yes… oh, yes.'

Guido drew in a deep raking breath, amazed at the relief he felt at her simple yes. His dark eyes slid over her. She was stunning, exquisite, with a perfect body and a long-limbed grace that drove him wild. His impulse was to simply grab her and drive straight into her, but instead he controlled his raging libido and gently lifted her in his arms to lay her on the bed.

He wanted to savour the moment, savour every inch of her… He had waited too long to hurry now. Lying down beside her, he raised himself on one elbow, placing his other hand on her flat stomach. For an instant a memory of the child that might have been flashed in his mind. Shaking his dark head, he stroked his hand up over her midriff to cup one perfect breast and let his fingers squeeze and tease the rigid nipple. He felt the shivers of excitement arrow through her body and knew this was all that mattered—not the past or the future, but now…

'Guido…' she moaned, a slender hand reaching to clasp his shoulder, digging into his firm flesh, urging him closer. He looked deep into her brilliant blue eyes and obliged, dipping his dark head to brush her lush lips, then moving lower to take the other taut nipple into his mouth.

For Sara it was like being set free from years of captivity. Her slender body strummed with sensation, and her long legs involuntarily parted, wanting him between them. Her back arched from the bed as he tasted and suckled her breasts, while her own hands delighted in the feel of his satin-smooth skin beneath her fingers as she traced over sleek, hard muscle and sinew.

He was everything she remembered and more. She rejoiced in the strength of his big powerful body over hers. Groaned out loud at the erotic touch of his tongue and teeth on her quivering body. The stroke of his hand moved up her thigh, to cup the most intimate part of her. Her legs moved restlessly wider in a silent plea for a yet more intimate touch, and skilfully he obliged.

She traced the length of his spine with ecstatic fingers, stroked the hard curve of his buttocks and found the rigid length of him with an eager if trembling hand.

'Wait…' Guido groaned, and rose up on to his knees.

She looked up into his darkly handsome face, at the night-black eyes burning with desire, and watched as he reached for the necessary and sheathed himself. Deep down inside she felt the tremors of need intensify to fever pitch. She opened her arms wide. 'Please.'

For a second Guido paused, catching his breath. Sara was exactly as he had pictured her in his imagination. Her fabulous body splayed beneath him on the bed, her arms and legs out-stretched, pleading… He leaned forward and ran his hands up over her legs, her inner thighs. She was wet and ready. But still he continued, along her flat stomach to her breasts, his fingers tracing the dusky pink areolae. Unable to resist the temptation, the need clawing at his gut, he bent his head and drew a pouting nipple into his mouth to suckle the tender tip. Then, unable to control his own ferocious desire a moment longer, in one lithe movement he settled between her thighs, his strong hands grasping her slim hips, and drove into her with one long, strong thrust.

She winced and, sensing her reaction, Guido paused. 'No—please don't stop,' she pleaded.

'Never,' Guido grated, and moved slowly, purposefully, a little at a time, until with one final sleek thrust he filled her to the hilt, and then withdrew, then moved again and again.

For Sara the incredible tension inside her exploded after the first few powerful strokes of his strong hard flesh, and her body convulsed in wave after wave of ecstatic release. Boneless and shaking in the wondrous aftermath, she was surprised as he continued to plunge deep inside her, then amazed as the exquisite tension spiralled all over again.

Her body moved in an answering rhythm to his as he thrust faster and faster, drove her mad with excitement again, possessing her completely, driving her until she reached a peak of pleasure that was so intense it was almost pain. She vaguely heard Guido cry out loud, felt his great body buck, and helplessly her inner muscles quivered and jerked in a storm of mindless pleasure.

Sara lay flat on her back, Guido on top of her, but his weight didn't register—only the musky male scent and strength of his body. She strung her arm around his shoulders, closed her eyes and sighed a deep sigh of utter contentment, her body sated and her mind blank.

Guido eased up, dislodging her arm from his shoulder. He heard her mumble and looked down at her. Her eyes were closed, her soft pink lips swollen from his kisses and her glorious hair a tangled mass across the pillow. He smiled, smoothed her tumbled hair back from her brow and rolled off the bed.

CHAPTER SEVEN

GUIDO walked into the *en-suite* bathroom and dispensed with the condom. He glanced in the vanity mirror and rubbed a hand across his jaw. Sara had very delicate skin; he could do with a shave before making love to her again.

He frowned. He didn't make love. He had sex. Admittedly with Sara incredibly satisfying, mind-blowing sex, but that was all it was. Sex… And he intended to continue having sex with her until he rid himself of this sudden inconvenient fascination for the woman. But not right now. He had some calls to make…

Back in business mode, he picked up a robe and shrugged into it before walking into the bedroom. He glanced at Sara, a smile of sheer male satisfaction curving his firm mouth. Her eyes were still closed. She appeared to be asleep, or more likely too embarrassed to face him—but, *Dio*, either way she was beautiful, the most fantastically responsive lover he had ever known. She was also the woman who'd run out on him, he reminded himself, and abruptly he turned and headed for the sitting room.

He picked up the house phone and ordered coffee, then plugged in his laptop and began to work. But ten minutes later he was staring at the screen, having accomplished nothing. Something niggled at the back of his mind... Who was he kidding? It was someone...Sara.

Then it registered that he had been so primed to get her into bed he had not thought of anything else. But now he *had* thought about it he allowed that this afternoon, when he had questioned her on her company and her abilities, if it had been anyone else he would have been impressed.

Recalling how she had completed university, worked in the City and then become a partner in Thompson & Beecham, he realised something did not add up. She could not have built a successful career without a lot of hard work. Yet Sara herself had confirmed his belief that she had blown the money she had demanded from his father on enjoying herself. But that could not be strictly true or she would not be where she was today.

So, okay, she had got away with a quarter of a million pounds—chickenfeed to Guido. If he was honest he had spent as much and more on quite a few other women who had occupied his bed over the years. But it had been the principle he had deplored at the time, and her method— threatening his family with scandal, saying she would go to the press with her accusations that Caterina had pushed her. It had been outrageous behaviour. But given she had been pregnant with his child, and had then miscarried, losing a year out of university, the money she had demanded was pitiful enough recompense. He ignored the uneasy twinge of guilt the thought aroused. In fact she had shown remarkable strength of character to achieve as much as she had.

He picked up the phone again, and this time ordered champagne…

When Sara had run out on him she had been very young, he reasoned, and with no family to support her he could hardly blame her for demanding money to get started again. She was back in his bed now. He could afford to be magnanimous and forget the past—and celebrate a new mature relationship with no unreasonable expectations on either side.

Sara slowly opened her eyes. Oh, God! What had she done? She silently groaned, and dragged the sheet up over her naked body. How could she have succumbed to Guido so easily? The lethargy and the pleasurable ache in certain parts of her anatomy answered for her. She had never felt more ashamed of herself in her life.

She had closed her eyes when Guido went to the bathroom, too mortified to look at him, and had kept them closed until she'd heard the bedroom door close behind him. She could not face him.

Ten years of celibacy and she had gone off like a firecracker in his arms. But if she was honest with herself she had to admit it wasn't solely her long-dormant sex life that was responsible for her reaction to Guido. She only had to be in the same room as him to feel the simmering tension, the sexual memory that connected them. He just had to look at her a certain way and her heart raced. She was powerless to control the excitement that bubbled up inside her. Whereas he had no such problem. He had made love to her with a sensual expertise she could only marvel at, but he had never lost control. He had got what he wanted, rolled off the bed and walked away without a word.

Blinking back tears of pain and anger, she sat up. She had to get a grip, cultivate a sophisticated shell in his presence to protect herself. She refused to be a victim yet again. Spying her briefs and bra on the floor, she leapt off the bed and picked them up. She pulled on her briefs and struggled to fasten her bra behind her back, her eyes searching the floor at the same time for her dress.

'Need some help?'

She spun around at the sound of Guido's voice. 'Not from you,' she snapped. He was walking towards her, a broad smile on his face and a bottle of champagne and two glasses in his hand. Six feet two of virile, macho male, wearing a loosely belted white robe that ended at mid-thigh and revealed an awful lot of his long muscular legs, Sara noted. She swallowed hard and raised her head.

His eyes met hers, and she saw the sensual gleam in the black depths. She had to fight down a sudden rush of heat to her cheeks as an unwanted vision of his totally naked body joined intimately with hers flashed in her mind. The breath stopped in her throat and she couldn't speak as she battled against the heat curling in her belly.

'Not the warm welcome I was expecting after the hot time we just had,' he quipped. 'But I have the remedy here.' Placing the bottle and glasses on the bedside table, Guido caught her shoulders and pulled the bra straps down her arms, dropping the scrap of lace on the floor.

'Much better,' he stated, his dark gaze lingering on her high firm breasts. 'Before was just the starter. Now I am hungry for the main course.' Guido looked at her stunned red face, a gleam of amusement lighting his eyes. 'You look shocked, Sara—yet we both know once was never enough in that respect. I have not changed, and if the present state of your delectable breasts is any indicator, neither have you.'

Sara heard his husky chuckle and to her horror found he was right. She had not thought straight since he'd walked back into the bedroom, and hastily she crossed her arms over her breasts and lurched back a step.

It would be futile to deny he turned her on—he always had. He was a handsome, powerful man who could turn any female on with one look from his sinfully sexy eyes. But she was no longer the gullible fool she had once been. And she had not forgotten why she was here.

'Sexually, maybe not—but I'm much more discerning now,' she said bluntly, finally finding her voice. 'A man who has to blackmail a woman into bed is not my idea of a lover.'

'Oh, come on, Sara.' Guido smiled, his gleaming eyes sweeping the mass of hair tumbling over her shoulders, the primly crossed arms over her breasts and lower, to where her skimpy briefs hugged her slender hips. 'You don't believe that. You're simply using it as an excuse for enjoying what we shared without having to admit you wanted me as much as I wanted you…still do.'

He was so obvious, Sara thought bitterly, anger overcoming her embarrassment at her near naked state. He stood there smiling, all testosterone-fuelled urbane male, with an expression of eager anticipation in his smouldering eyes. Confident she would fall back into his arms like a ripe plum. Well, he was in for one heck of a shock.

'Control your enthusiasm,' she said with saccharine sweetness. 'If what you say is true and there is no blackmail involved,' she said, lifting cold blue eyes to his, refusing to be intimidated, 'then I can trust you to keep your deal with Pat and Dave.' Casually she turned slightly and took a sheet from the bed to wrap sarong-style around her body. She could do the sophisticated lover when she tried, she told herself, and glanced back at Guido. 'Yes?' she prompted with a sardonic lift of one perfectly shaped eyebrow.

Guido's magnanimity faded fast as it finally dawned on him that the cold-eyed woman staring back at him as if he was something she had found under a stone was not the exhausted woman he had left in bed sated by sex. He had been willing to forgive her past behaviour, prepared to treat her as he would any other adult lover, but not any more…

'There we might have a problem… But you are an intelligent woman, Sara, and I'm sure you understand it is good business practice to always have an edge when making a deal,' he prompted silkily. 'I want you as my lover—a position I know you are not averse to filling after the last hour.'

'You blackmailed me,' she responded flatly. But why, oh, why had she let him? She inwardly cringed with embarrassment at her own wanton behaviour. If she had just left when she'd had the chance—run out on him instead of being determined to match him in a mature business discussion—she wouldn't be in this mess. But then she would never have experienced the incredible pleasure of his great body thrusting deep inside her, a traitorous little voice whispered in her head.

At the same time Guido declared, '*Blackmail* is such a harsh word, Sara.'

His dark insolent eyes mocked her. He knew as well as she did that thoughts of Pat and Dave had been the last thing on her mind from the moment his lips had met hers. Her fingers curled tighter in the sheet she was holding, tension in every line of her slender body.

'I prefer to call it hedging my bets. So I suggest you and I have a relationship for…say a year?' He shrugged one elegant shoulder. 'Or less if we grow tired of the arrangement. And in return I guarantee Pat and Dave their contract for one year. How does that sound?'

He knew damn fine how it sounded, Sara thought, anger and bitterness welling up inside her all over again. She had been right all along. But ranting at the man was not going to make any difference. If she wanted to make sure her friends and their unborn child had a happy, worry-free pregnancy and birth, did she have a choice?

Her mind spun, going over everything Guido had said since they had met again, everything he had done, seeking an escape. If it had just been Pat and Dave she could have walked away without too much soul-searching. They were her friends but mature enough to take care of themselves. It was their unborn child that tugged at her heartstrings.

She would help them financially herself if she could. But while she earned a reasonable income, she had very little spare cash and they needed a lot. Pity she didn't know another philanthropic millionaire…

Out of nowhere a stray thought came unbidden to her mind. 'Wait a minute—how did you know Peter Wells had gone to Hong Kong?' she demanded.

'His boss, Mark Hanlom, is a business associate of mine,' he responded smoothly.' 'I might have mentioned I had met Wells and was impressed by his financial talent, and I might have suggested his expertise could be utilised to much better effect in the Far East.'

'You got rid of him!' Sara exclaimed.

'That sounds harsh—a bit like a Mafioso don wiping out the opposition.' Guido chuckled. 'When actually I did the boy a favour by furthering his career.'

'And of course your motive was as pure as the

driven snow?' She sneered. 'Not just a way to get rid of my—lover.' She hesitated for a split second on the lie. 'But then I shouldn't be surprised—any man who would stoop to blackmail to get a woman in his bed is hardly going to baulk at getting rid of a lover.'

'Oh, please, Sara—save me from the holier than thou routine,' Guido drawled sardonically. 'You had no qualms in demanding money from my father so you could get out of our marriage and line your pockets at the same time.'

'Me blackmail you? Are you out of your mind?' Sara exclaimed bristling with rage, her laser-like glance full of bitterness. 'Your father insisted I take the cheque and demanded I leave immediately. He threatened me if I refused.'

'Threatened you with what?' Guido mocked. He was fast losing his patience at her blind insistence that somehow he and his family had mistreated her. She had been cosseted in the lap of luxury compared to what she'd been used to. She had always had insecurities—a hangover from the time she had spent in foster homes after her mother died, he supposed. He could understand it, in a way, but he was damned if he was going to allow her to continue to view his family with the same fear and contempt she carried for those who had mistreated her while she was in care. 'Bread and water?'

'Nothing so crude. He told me that with the baby gone there was no reason for me to stay. You had only married me because I was pregnant, and you wanted out of the marriage.' Sara hesitated, reluctant to reveal the clincher— and then thought, why not? She had nothing to hide. 'What with my obvious unstable emotional state, as evidenced by my supposedly paranoid dislike of Caterina—which, given that I didn't know my father might be a genetic condition, he insisted I take the money and leave,' she ended sarcastically.

Guido's dark eyes narrowed on her flushed, defiant face. She actually looked as if she believed what she was saying. She was right in one respect, he realised rather belatedly. Being brutally honest, at twenty-four marriage had been the last thing on his mind, and he *had* married her mainly because she was pregnant.

For the first time in years he began to doubt what his father had told him. Then he remembered the letter she had left him.

'Come off it, Sara—I read the note you left. Spare me more of your stories. I am not interested. It does not matter any more. The here and now is all that concerns me.'

Sara shook her head. 'You're amazing. You see nothing wrong in what you did to me.'

Guido shrugged his shoulders, his darkly handsome face hard. 'I never harmed a hair of your head—not then and not now,' he said flatly, frustration riding him at her insistence on raking over the past. 'You enjoyed every minute you spent in my bed this afternoon, so don't bother denying the obvious,' he declared, with a sardonic lift of an ebony brow. 'And as for Wells...I simply did him a favour and got rid of the competition at the same time.' Picking up the bottle of champagne, he added, 'I suggest we agree to disagree on what happened in the past, and have a nice non-controversial toast—a drink to success in our new relationship.'

He was so damn blasé. The past meant

nothing to him. *She* meant nothing to him other than a female body to warm his bed for a while. There was no point in arguing with him. Suddenly Sara felt seriously afraid. Her guarded blue eyes swept over him. He was in the process of opening the bottle of champagne and of course the cork popped perfectly—he didn't spill a drop…

Guido was so damn arrogant, so confident in his ability to get what he wanted—in his business life and his private life. He was clever, cunning, and surprisingly patient—and all at once she knew how a fly must feel, captured in the skilfully spun web of a spider. Guido was just as dark and just as lethal…

And if she wasn't very careful he would devour her whole.

'Here.' He walked to where she stood and lifted a glass full of sparkling champagne. 'Take it, Sara.'

She took the glass from his hand, the slight brush of his fingers on hers sending an electric charge the length of her arm. Quickly she raised the glass to her lips and took a long drink. She needed it.

'To us,' he murmured, the corners of his mouth quirking in the hint of a smile, 'and to a mutually satisfying affair. Agreed?'

There it was… Yes or no…

Sara took another long slug of the champagne, draining her glass, and walked past him to deposit the empty glass on the bedside table, giving herself time to think. Turning slowly, she tightened her grip on the sheet. It took a terrific effort of will to look back at him. Not helped by the fact he looked incredibly sexy, with his robe hanging open to reveal his broad, slightly hair-roughened chest.

'Perhaps.' She affected a casual shrug, keeping her blue eyes fixed on his face in the hope it would be less distracting than his sleek, toned body. But inside she was seething with a mixture of emotions. The uppermost one, to her shame, was not anger at Guido's blackmail but a deep-rooted desire to experience the wonder of his possession all over again.

She knew it was foolish… She knew it was dangerous…

She also knew it was inescapable if she

wanted to protect her friends. But this time Guido was not going to have everything his own way. This time she was going to play him at his own game and set a few guidelines of her own.

'If I agree, first I want to hear from Pat's own lips that they have got their money within the next fourteen days. Secondly I want it clearly understood that our arrangement can't interfere with my career or my everyday life,' she said, affecting a cool sophistication she was far from feeling. 'I will meet you only when you are in England and at a convenient time for me, which will have to be at the weekend. I have worked too long and too hard to jeopardise my business with what can only be a casual affair for no longer than twelve months.'

'I couldn't have put it better myself.' Guido grinned and in two lithe strides was beside her and refilling their glasses. Placing hers in her hand, he added, 'A toast to us and a very English weekend affair—yes.'

Looking up at him, big and dark, with the light of triumph gleaming in his eyes, Sara nodded her head and said, 'Yes.' She touched her glass to his, a slightly caustic smile curving her lush lips, and drained the glass.

Guido had got what he wanted—as always, she thought acidly. She wasn't in the least surprised he had agreed to her terms. After all he had a lover in America and another in Hong Kong that she knew about, and probably more.

There was no pretence. He wanted her for sex. There was no possibility of deluding herself into thinking it was anything more. For which she should be grateful…

Guido let out a long breath of relief while not admitting for a moment he had doubted what her answer would be. He removed the glass from her hand and deposited it beside his on the table.

'A kiss to seal the deal,' he drawled softly, his dark gaze raking over her in possessive male appraisal. She was his—every delectable inch of her. He reached for her slender shoulders and drew her into his arms. He saw the brief flicker of resistance in her brilliant blue eyes and wasted no more time. He lowered his proud dark head and covered her luscious mouth with his own.

What was the common cliché? 'Lie back and

think of England?' Yes, she could do that, Sara thought as his lips brushed hers.

And it was the last clear thought she would have for some time…

His tongue dipped into her mouth and he kissed her with a passionate intensity that made her senses swirl and her brain turn to mush.

A low moan escaped her as his mouth left hers to suck lightly on the pulse beating madly in the curve of her neck. A strong hand stroked down over her buttocks and pressed her closer, and she was made vitally aware of the hard strength of his arousal. She melted against him, heat pooling between her thighs.

He lifted his head, his black eyes burning down at her.

'I should go now…' She made a last-gasp protest, but her hands of their own volition lifted to curve around his neck, and she was oblivious to the sheet falling at her feet.

'I was hoping for the opposite.' Guido chuckled—a deep, throaty sound—and, shrugging off his robe, tumbled her back onto the bed.

Sara's lips twitched with laughter. He was so

dazzlingly gorgeous, so very male, she thought helplessly, her blue eyes roaming avidly over every rippling muscle and sinew of his great body, and she drew in a shaky breath and stretched out her arms to him.

'Patience, Sara.' He smiled—a slow, sensuous curl of his firm lips—and, leaning over her, caught her hands in his, kissed each palm, and lifted them above her head.

She looked up into his taut handsome face, saw the lusty intent in his night-black eyes, and every nerve in her body tightened in fierce anticipation, excitement sizzling through her.

'I promised myself this from the minute I saw you again,' he declared throatily, and in one swift move flipped her on her stomach.

Promised what? she wondered. And tried to push up, but his mouth closed over one small ear.

'Humour me,' he murmured, and nuzzled the curve of her throat.

The warmth of his breath, the subtle caress, and Sara was weak and hot with longing to the exclusion of all else.

He ran his hands up over her buttocks,

kneading gently, then followed the indentation of her waist. She felt the rasping touch of his tongue between her shoulderblades as a strong hand slipped beneath her, stroking over her breasts, settling low on her belly. Long fingers curled in the soft curls at the apex of her thighs, skilfully delving between the velvet folds to tease and pleasure her hot, moist feminine core.

She could not see him, could not touch him, but the feelings and sensations he ignited in her trembling body made her groan out loud. She felt the slide of his tongue down her spine and exquisite sensations quivered through her in an unstoppable tide. His sinfully clever fingers caressed the most sensitive intimate parts of her, and at the same time his sensuous mouth traced a string of kisses down her spine.

She writhed wildly beneath him, abandoning herself to the incredible sensations roaring like a firestorm of heat and desire through her body.

Vaguely she heard Guido groan. 'I dreamt of this…' And felt his tongue trace circles in her burning flesh. But his fingers never stopped their expert caresses. Tension, excitement spiralled inside her, enflaming her hunger, her need, to a fever-pitch of almost torturous pleasure. A high, whimpering cry escaped her, and in a lithe movement she was on her back, her legs tugged either side of Guido's strong thighs.

Her wild passion-hazed gaze sought his. He was kneeling over her, his eyes deep pits of molten passion. His hands grasped her slender hips and lifted her into his lap. Her body arched like a bowstring, her head fell back and she reached for him with clawing, desperate hands, wrapping her arms around his neck as he drove up into her with a hard deep thrust that sent her soaring with fierce need and frantic excitement ever higher. The repeated thrust of his powerful body stretched and filled her, his strong hands moulding her, tumbling her on the bed in a frantic coupling as he moved harder and faster, the rhythm increasing to fever-pitch until fierce spasms of excruciating pleasure engulfed her and her whole being was reduced to one of sublime sensation…

CHAPTER EIGHT

A LONG time later Sara felt the brush of a hand against her hair and slowly opened her eyes.

'That was amazing.' Guido grinned up at her.

'Guido…' she murmured. She was lying on top of him, her head resting on his broad shoulder. She could feel the rapid beat of his heart against her own. She smiled and, lifting a slender finger, lovingly traced the line of his jaw, the curve of his wickedly sexy mouth.

'Sublime,' she said softly, her body throbbing with the wondrous joy of sexual release. 'But what was it you promised yourself?' she prompted, recalling his impassioned words.

A smile of pure satisfaction curved his firm mouth. 'Can't you guess, sweetheart? From the minute I saw you lying on your stomach on that yacht…' a caressing hand stroked down her back, and long fingers settled at the base of her spine '...I promised myself I would kiss your delectable dimples once more.'

'You, sir, have a dimple fetish,' Sara teased, wallowing in the languorous aftermath of their lovemaking.

'Only with you, Sara, only with you.' He chuckled.

'Then I approve,' she murmured, totally satisfied, and glanced around. 'We are upside down on the bed. How did that happen?'

Guido rolled her over onto her back, and reared up on one elbow to look down at her. Sara, with her hair a silken mass about her shoulders, her lush mouth swollen from his kisses and her creamy breasts bearing the marks of his hungry mouth, was a vision to behold.

'Give me ten minutes and I will show you,' he offered, but his stomach chose that moment to give a distinctive rumble and a wry smile twisted his lips. 'Make that half an hour. Unlike you, I missed lunch.' He grinned, and then grimaced as the ringing of a cellphone cut through the intimate atmosphere. 'Sorry.' He leapt off the bed. 'I need to answer that.'

Dreamily Sara watched him walk stark naked to extract his cellphone from his jacket, lying among the mess of clothes on the floor. Watched him straighten up, heard his staccato voice answer, and saw his handsome face harden. And suddenly she shivered, a chill invading her very bones.

For long blissful minutes she had forgotten the last decade—forgotten they were divorced. Seduced all over again by his great body and his incredible sexual expertise, not once but twice. If she lay here a moment longer more than likely thrice…

Hastily she scrambled off the bed and quickly picked her briefs and bra off the floor.

'Sara.' She froze at the sound of her name.

'Yes?' She made herself look up at him with a forced smile, and though she longed to cover herself she knew if she was to have any chance of getting through this affair with her heart intact she had to be as bold and sophisticated as Guido.

How did a man manage to look like the consummate business tycoon stark naked with a phone in one hand and the evidence of his latest sexual experience in the other? Sara wondered. Yet somehow Guido achieved the feat, with a staggering nonchalance she could only marvel at.

'I have to take this call.' He indicated the house phone with a nod of his dark head. 'Ring Room Service and order me a couple of sandwiches and a coffee, sweetheart.' And without waiting for her answer he walked across to the bathroom, the phone glued to his ear.

What did your last slave die of? Sara wanted to yell. But instead she swiftly slipped on her briefs and bra and picked up the phone. It could have been worse; he could have asked her to get rid of the condom, she supposed, as she placed the order. Then she sprang into action.

Two minutes later she had retrieved her bag and sandals from the sitting room, and was picking her dress up off the floor just as Guido walked out of the bathroom, still talking on his cellphone.

Thank heaven he had draped a towel around his lean hips. Straightening up, she shot him a brief glance as she walked past him.

'My turn,' she mouthed, darting into the bathroom and closing the door behind her.

She stared at her reflection in the mirror and barely recognised herself. What had she done? Her hair was all over the place, her lips were swollen, and a few red marks marred the smooth skin of her neck and her breasts. It was pretty obvious, she thought wryly, and set about repairing the damage as best she could. When she walked back into the bedroom once more, outwardly she was the smartly dressed woman who had arrived a few hours earlier. But inwardly she was a quivering mass of warring emotions.

Guido was still on the phone, but he broke off long enough to arch a black brow in her direction. 'You're dressed.'

'Yes, well, I don't want to give the waiter an eyeful when he delivers your order,' she quipped.

Guido grinned, and Sara headed for the sitting room.

The food arrived, and Sara paced the elegant room, waiting for Guido. Realising what she was doing, she sat down on a sofa and poured a cup of coffee. She had paced the floor enough for Guido in the past. Never again.

When he joined her, now thankfully wearing a towelling robe, she had her wayward emotions under control.

'Sorry about that, Sara,' he murmured, dropping a swift kiss on the top of her head and lowering his long body down beside her. 'But it was important.' Tucking into the sandwiches, between bites he explained, 'Unfortunately I have to be in Hong Kong by tomorrow afternoon, and as they are eight hours ahead I will have to leave later tonight.'

'I understand,' she said smoothly, picking up her bag and rising to her feet. 'As it happens I have an appointment this evening at eight with a client. I really have to get going.'

'Isn't that rather late?' Guido paused, the sandwich halfway to his mouth, his earlier complete satisfaction fading somewhat as he looked up at her.

'Oh, come on, Guido—I'm sure *you* have business dinners.'

He could not argue with that. But he wanted

to. 'Yes, of course. But I'm surprised you booked a business lunch and a dinner on the same day. I thought you women were always watching your figures.'

Sara gave a light laugh. 'Actually, it's not a dinner. My client owns a nightclub, and his work day starts at eight in the evening. I'm meeting him at his club.'

Guido frowned. Dropping the half-eaten sandwich back on the plate, he felt a weird sensation tightening his chest.

Indigestion, impatience, anger—or the green-eyed monster jealousy…something he had never experienced before and did not want to recognise now…

'A nightclub?' he said bluntly.

'Yes—you know, those places where people go to dance and enjoy themselves? The places you frequent quite often, if the gossip columns are to be believed. I'll give you my new phone number.' Taking a card from her purse, she handed it to him. 'Give me a call when you get back.'

Guido grimaced and stood up to look down into her guileless blue eyes. Of course what she said was perfectly reasonable. And he did have to leave later anyway. But he had hoped… 'Wait till I dress and I'll get a cab and take you home.'

'Really there's no need,' she insisted and, reaching up, pulled his head down to press a quick kiss on his mouth.

He lifted a hand to pull her close; perhaps what he hoped for wasn't going to elude him after all? But just as quickly she tried to move away. He hauled her back and kissed her with a ruthless and possessive passion. When he felt her soft and yielding, trembling in his arms, only then did he raise his head.

He saw the tumult in her incredible blue eyes and offered her a mocking smile. 'In case you had any doubt, Sara.' He brushed a stray tendril of hair from her brow. 'That was a reminder that you are mine for the next twelve months, and don't you forget it.' Only then did he set her free.

'As if I could,' he thought he heard her whisper as she turned to open the door. She stopped and glanced back at him. 'Have a good trip, Guido.'

The twisted smile she gifted him was still bothering him long after she had gone.

* * *

The first thing Sara did when she got back to the safety of her own apartment was to call Pat, and when she put the phone down ten minutes later she knew her fate was sealed. Pat and Dave were counting on Guido's support and thought it was a done deal. They were preparing to sail the ship to Naples even as they spoke. Sara hadn't had the heart to disillusion her friend and tell her he was a black-mailing skunk.

But it wasn't skunk she scented when she stripped off her clothes in her bedroom. It was the tantalisingly musky male scent of Guido on her skin. She stepped into the shower, letting the warm spray gush over her, and then proceeded to wash every inch of her tingling flesh. But however hard she tried she could not wash away what he made her feel.

Crawling into bed, she burrowed down under the cover, subconsciously trying to hide from her tormenting thoughts. Tears of pain and anger burned the backs of her eyes, but she refused to let them fall. She had cried enough tears over Guido years ago...she wasn't about to do so again. As for the anger, she sadly realized, turning restlessly in her bed, it was as much with herself as with Guido Barberi. Because despite his devious games, his blackmail, there was one undeniable truth: she still wanted him. She wanted to feel again the magic of his possession. She could not help herself.

When was blackmail not blackmail? When the woman was a willing partner? At least it was only for twelve months at most, she consoled herself. But deep down in her innermost being she knew that was no consolation at all...

At work the next morning when Billy Johnson called to arrange a meeting Sara was on the point of turning him down. But she changed her mind. She was stuck with seeing Guido for as long as it suited him, so why shouldn't she make some money out of it...?

On a Friday evening almost four weeks later Sara walked back into the hotel and ignored the smirking receptionist as she signed in and took a key. Guido had called earlier and told her he would be delayed, and to wait for him in his suite.

She had tried to argue, but his response had been, 'Damn it, Sara, do as I say. I'm late enough already without you giving me grief.' And he'd put the phone down.

She let herself into the suite and headed straight for the bedroom. Dropping her over-night bag on the bed, she glanced around. The scene of her downfall…

When Guido had returned from Hong Kong that first Friday evening she had met him here, and she had not left the suite until early Monday morning. Even then Guido had tried to talk her into staying until Monday night, as he'd been spending the day in his London office.

She had refused, sticking to her weekends only deal. It was the only way she could retain some slight control over the affair. She certainly could not control her wayward body. Guido made love to her with a seemingly insatiable powerful passion that drove her wild and to the point of exhaustion. And yet as each weekend passed her hunger for him grew. She hardly knew herself any more.

A wry smile curved her lips. She had become a sex addict—at least she hoped that was true. Anything deeper would be an absolute disaster.

Last weekend when he had asked her to join him in Italy she had refused, so he had joined her here. Then to her surprise he had taken her out to dinner, and Pat and Dave had joined them. Her friends were delighted the deal had gone through, and it had been a celebration. Only Sara had known it was Guido's way of showing her he had kept his part of the deal to the letter and he expected her to do the same. Which she had, by spending the Saturday night and most of Sunday in his bed, before he'd left for New York.

Now Sara sighed and, crossing to the *en-suite* bathroom, shed her clothes. After a quick shower she returned to the bedroom. She drew a blue satin nightgown from her bag and slipped it on—a present from Guido—then walked back into the sitting room to wait… Primed and ready for his delectation she thought, not liking the cynical woman she had become.

* * *

Guido strode over to the reception desk and booked in. He was frustrated, tired and angry. He had expected to arrive at six, but it was now ten in the evening. He had called Sara and told her he was going to be delayed, told her to wait at the hotel for him.

'Has my guest arrived?' he demanded of the receptionist.

'Miss Beecham? Yes, sir.'

'Very good. We will only be staying one night—not three, as planned,' he informed the young man before he turned and headed for the elevator.

He rubbed a weary hand through his hair and leant back against the wall. This English affair he had agreed to with Sara was playing havoc with his business life. This was the third weekend in a row he had flown to London, and it was damned inconvenient. Tomorrow he was taking ownership of an apartment in Mayfair which would make things easier. He disliked living out of a suitcase. But it wouldn't completely solve the problem.

He had tried to get Sara to agree to join him in Italy last week, but she had flatly refused. She was everything he wanted in his bed, but she was as stubborn as a mule when it came to altering their deal. He had flown back to London last Saturday with Dave and Pat in tow when they could so much more easily have met in Naples, where Dave had berthed the ship. Then on Sunday evening he had flown to New York until Tuesday, and the last three days he had spent back in Naples while his father had undergone massive heart surgery in a last-ditch attempt to correct his damaged heart.

But it was the conversation he had had with Aldo the night before his father's operation that was really preying on his mind. He did not know what or whom to believe any more.

Sara heard the door and rose gracefully to her feet, fixing a smile on her face when inside she was seething that he was hours late.

Guido dropped his bag on the floor and strode towards her, all vibrant and powerful male.

'So you finally made it?' she said lightly, and wondered if his lawyer lover had delayed him in New York. But she let none of her jealous resentment show as she lifted her face for his kiss.

'Sorry, sweetheart, the delay was unavoidable.' And, looping an arm around her waist, he drew her into the warmth of his body, his mouth seeking hers and kissing her with a deep, almost desperate passion that she was helpless to deny.

'I had to cut short my stay in New York and stay in Naples for a few days while my father had heart surgery. Luckily it was successful.'

So he hadn't been with Margot all week. Sara hated herself for the relief she felt. As for his father—she was surprised he had mentioned him. Their relationship was not geared towards anything personal, simply sex. Guido never spoke about his family and she never asked.

Sara did not want to feel sorry for Guido , and his father certainly did not deserve her sympathy, but, looking up into his handsome face, she saw the lines of tiredness around his eyes, the grimness of his mouth. Up close, he actually looked like hell.

'He is fine now, and Aldo sends his regards.'

'That was nice of him,' she said quietly.

'Yes, well, Aldo is a nice man.' Guido grimaced. 'A lot nicer than me, it would seem.

Do me a favour and get me a whisky and soda and bring it through. I need a shower.' And he strode off into the bedroom.

Discarding his clothing, he realised Sara had carefully avoided offering any sympathy for his father. He should have been angry, but then Sara had never offered any condolences when he had told her Caterina was dead, and after what Aldo had told him he wasn't surprised.

Stepping into the shower, he turned the jets on full and, closing his eyes, threw back his proud head and let the water stream down his face. He wished like hell he had never mentioned meeting Sara again to his brother.

For once in his life his supreme belief, his confidence in his ability to read any situation, had taken an almighty blow. According to Aldo, Sara had been a good friend to him and Marta years ago. She had often taken the two teenagers out in the car Guido had put at her disposal so they could meet without the rest of the family knowing. Mainly because Caterina had threatened Aldo that she would reveal his youthful relationship with the daughter of the local bar owner to his father. According to Caterina the girl was far beneath him in social standing.

Which had been rich, Aldo had laughed, given the rumours of Caterina's relationship with the married gardener that had abounded after Sara had lost her baby. But Guido had not been amused. He had never heard any rumours—but then he had been working eighteen-hour days.

Then Aldo had told him quite casually that he had been blind where Caterina was concerned. He didn't blame Guido, because he knew Guido had been only six when Caterina—a year younger—had come to live with the family, and Guido had grown up accustomed to her unadulterated hero-worship. In fact Aldo had said in his opinion it was probably the reason why Guido treated the women in his life so casually today. He expected adoration without having to make any effort.

For Guido, hearing a few home truths from his kid brother had not been a pleasant experience, and it had got worse…

Aldo reckoned Caterina had always seen herself as the much loved baby of the family, and everyone in the family had encouraged her belief. When Aldo had arrived four years later she must have bitterly resented the new baby. Aldo had grasped at a young age that she was jealous of him—in fact she'd actively disliked him—and he had quickly learnt to keep out of her way. She'd only been nice to him when Guido was around, and he was amazed Guido had never noticed the girl was totally possessive of him.

Guido had laughed and said, 'Come on, Aldo— she was like a sister to me. Nothing more.'

Guido groaned and opened his eyes, recalling Aldo's response.

'Some sister. I saw you kissing her the New Year's Eve before you went to London, and there was nothing sisterly about her. She was almost devouring you whole. She was furious when you came home with your young pregnant bride, and she behaved like an absolute cow to Sara, making her life a misery when you weren't around. She had a vicious streak a mile wide. Remember the puppy I got for my eighth birthday? Well, I was chasing him around the outside of the house one day, and as I turned the corner I saw Caterina walk out of the door and kick him off the terrace with a right footer that would have made the legendary Pele jealous. I took him to the vet and he diagnosed fractured ribs.'

Guido had listened in growing dismay as Aldo continued.

'After Sara lost the baby Marta and I sneaked in to see her in hospital. I gave Sara the benefit of my experience in avoiding conflict with Caterina and Dad. She was genuinely afraid of the pair of them, and I'm not surprised she ran away. That is all I'm saying.' And Aldo had walked away.

Guido respected his younger brother, though he was nothing like him in nature. Aldo had been fascinated by trucks and the trucking firm since childhood, and had never once considered doing anything else with his life. He had fallen in love at fifteen, stayed true to the girl, and was now happily married. He ran the largest part of the transport side of the business from the Naples office supremely well, and was totally happy with his life. He was not given to flights of fancy, so Guido had to consider what he had said.

He had spent a sleepless night. He had always considered Caterina as a sister, nothing more, but the long-forgotten memory of that New Year's Eve party, with Caterina kissing him passionately and suggesting they got together had surfaced in his mind. Then he had laughed at the idea, and put it down to the fact Caterina had drunk too much, but now he was not so sure… While he did not for one moment believe Caterina had pushed Sara down the steps, he could see she might have been consistently nasty to Sara, as Aldo had said. It was not surprising Sara had been confused and paranoid after her accident.

The next morning Guido hadn't been able to help himself, and had asked his father to tell him again what Sara had said when she'd left him. Maybe it had been because he was going into surgery, but his father had confessed that Sara had never actually demanded money to keep her mouth shut. He had made that up to make it easier for Guido to accept her leaving him. Sara had simply said the marriage had been a huge mistake, and had requested money only so she could go back to England and resume her life.

Guido could not get his head around the fact that he might have been wrong about Sara. As for Caterina—he didn't want to think about it. And, turning off the water, he stepped out of the shower.

CHAPTER NINE

'YOUR whisky, sir.' Sara was standing holding out a glass, her blue eyes gleaming appreciatively as they swept over his naked body.

She was wearing a blue satin gown that fell to her feet. Tiny straps looped over her slender shoulders, and the fine lace inset in the bodice plunged to her navel. Guido didn't think…

Taking the glass from her hand, he downed it in one go and curved his other hand around her waist to hold her. He placed the glass on the nearest flat service and, burrowing his hand through the silken mass of her hair, clasped her nape and bent his head, desperate to taste her luscious lips, to bury himself in her sexy body.

Lifting his head, he looked down into her sparkling eyes. 'I like the gown,' he husked, running a finger beneath a fine strap.

Sara was shocked, but breathless, the feel of his hot, wet body against her own igniting a burning heat inside her. 'You bought it for me,' she breathed, looking up into his dark face. She saw his desire—and something more she did not recognise.

The past two weekends Guido had presented her with quite a few pieces of outrageously expensive lingerie, and she wore them as some kind of defence against the overwhelming emotions he aroused in her. She only had to look at herself in the mirror to know it was not the real Sara who shared his bed and his body, simply the Sara he wanted her to be. In that way she kept a little of her true self back, but right at this moment holding back was the last thing on her mind...

'I have great taste,' he murmured. 'And, oh, *Dio*, I need the taste, the feel of you around me so badly.' He groaned, and the straps were slipped from her shoulders. His hands palmed her breasts as the gown slipped to pool at her feet.

He bent his dark head and he drew one perfect nipple into his mouth, rolling it around his tongue. Sara shuddered helplessly in response, her hands reaching around his broad shoulders, holding him to her as he bestowed the same pleasure on the other.

Instantly she was burning for him. His strong hands lifted her, his face a taut mask of passion as he backed her against the wall and wrapped her legs around his waist. Her fingers dug into his flesh, and she cried out as without any pre-liminaries he thrust into her hot, sleek body. Filling her, possessing her, driving her wild, until she convulsed around him as he spilled his seed inside her.

Slowly he lowered her to the ground, his arms folding around her. He rested his head against hers, his broad chest heaving. 'Did I hurt you?' he rasped.

Sara sighed—a long, shaky sound. All the times they had made love she had never known Guido to lose control until now. 'Surprised me, maybe. But hurt—no,' she murmured, and pressed her lips to his shoulder.

'Thank you, Sara.'

What was he thanking her for? she wondered,

and was still wondering when he carried her into the bedroom.

Guido laid her gently down on the bed and lay down beside her. Leaning over her, he brushed the silken mass of her hair back from her brow and slowly smoothed the long length across the pillow.

'I dream of your hair like this,' he murmured. 'I dream of your body like this.' And with tender, caressing hands he stroked her shoulders, her breasts, her stomach, her thighs—all the time dropping tiny kisses on her eyes, her nose, her lips, arousing her all over again.

What followed was the gentlest most erotic experience of her life. Lazily, with an almost worshipful adoration, Guido touched her, talked to her in husky words she did not understand but she sensed were heartfelt. She stroked his face, his back, all of him, with a freedom she had rarely allowed herself before, and the pleasure grew and grew. When they finally joined the slowly aroused rippling sensations increased to an incredible tension and then a mutual climax so intense Sara thought she would die from the pleasure. She stopped breathing for one blind, all-encompassing moment.

When she felt the wonderful, shuddering weight of Guido over her, she opened her eyes and saw his night-black eyes watching her with a curious, almost vulnerable intensity she had never seen before, and words of love and reassurance hovered on her lips...

Reassurance... The incongruous thought stopped the words of love she had so nearly uttered in her throat. This was Guido, her ex-husband, and blackmailing lover. He needed reassurance about as much as the devil himself did.

Was she mad? No, she realised with a sudden bittersweet anguish. Deep down inside, beneath the sophisticated image she portrayed for Guido, beneath the resentment and fear, she still loved him and probably always would. Everyone used to tell her she was like her petite blonde mother in nature, though she looked nothing like her. So maybe she was fated, like her mother, to only ever love one man. The thought gave her no joy...

'You're heavy,' she said, wriggling from

beneath him, and she did not mean just physically. Sara had a horrible conviction Guido would weigh heavy on her heart for all time, and she must never let him know.

'And you are heavenly,' he returned, wrapping an arm around her shoulders. He pulled her close to his long body, a long leg stretching over her thighs. 'I want to talk to you,' he said, and, cupping her chin in his hand, he looked down at her with dark, serious eyes.

'I spoke to Aldo when I was in Naples. He said to wish you all the best from him and Marta and to thank you again for helping them when they first got together.'

'That was nice of him,' Sara said guardedly, not knowing where this conversation was going.

'He also told me a few home truths. Apparently I was blind where Caterina was concerned. I lapped up her devoted cousin act without a second thought. But he knew a different Caterina… She didn't like him because he'd usurped her place as the baby in the family, and she was pretty nasty to him when I was not around.' Guido grimaced. 'He also said she was an absolute cow to you—his words—and he was not surprised when you ran back to England.' His dark intent eyes searched her face.

Sara said nothing and the silence lengthened.

'If that is true then it could have been instrumental in causing your confusion at the time. And I owe you an apology for not realising how badly Caterina behaved towards you, and for not taking care of you as I should have done as your husband,' Guido said finally.

She had to believe he meant what he was saying. She could see it in his solemn dark eyes. But she noted he didn't mention her claim that Caterina had pushed her down the steps. That he was never going to believe.

'Given Caterina is dead, it doesn't matter any more. So don't beat yourself up over it,' Sara said dryly.

'Is that all you have to say?'

'Yes. Now, if—' She tried to sit up.

'No—wait. I haven't finished. I have another confession to make.'

Her gaze rested on his stern features. He looked like a man who had bitten into a lemon and was determined to eat it, and she almost smiled. Guido trying to be humble was a sight to behold.

'I spoke to my father before he went into surgery, and he confessed that you never threatened to go to the press and repeat your accusations against Caterina to get money out of him. He made up the story for my sake—to make it easier for me to accept you had left me—and for that he apologised.'

'Did he now?' she commented with a scathing smile. 'I am so relieved.'

'Sarcasm does not become you, Sara. And to be fair you were quite economical with the truth when we met again. You said my father threatened you to get you to leave, and that never happened.'

She should have known Guido could not do the concerned, humble act for long. It wasn't in his character.

'Quite the reverse. He told me he tried to persuade you to stay—promised to do everything he could to make sure you were properly taken care of while I was away. But you insisted on leaving, and you asked him to give you the money to help you settle back in England. You could have just told me you wanted out, Sara. Maybe you were far too young to be married.' Thrusting herself away from him, Sara sat up. 'So let me get this straight. You no longer think I demanded money from the old man to keep my mouth shut?' She smiled slightly and let her eyes roam slowly over him. He was lying there, all unrepentant male, talking as though he was doing her a favour by admitting he had been *slightly* wrong about her. She could only marvel at his father's disingenuous but subtle explanation.

The old man had told Guido he'd said he would make sure she was properly taken care of, and that was precisely what he *had* said. There was no arguing with that. But he'd had his hand on the telephone to call the doctor at the time…

'You believe I left because I was too young to be married, and that I asked for the money to make a new start? Have I got that straight?'

'Yes. You took the money and left.'

'Do you remember the last day we spent together back then?' she asked, anger and bitterness rising like gall in her throat. She was going to have this out with him once and for all. 'I followed you to our bedroom after lunch, and you made love to me for the first time in over six weeks. Then Caterina walked in. She said she was sorry for intruding, but she was on her way to town and wanted to say goodbye to you before she left, as she knew you were flying off to New York that evening. Something you had omitted to tell me. We argued. You were furious at being found out, and later, when you were leaving, I broke down and cried and begged you to take me with you. You said no, and turned to your father. From the little Italian I could understand you asked him to take care of me. Then you told me that perhaps it would be beneficial for both of us to spend some time apart—that it would give me a chance to calm down—and you would call me when you were coming back.'

'You had only been out of hospital a short time and you were a bit hysterical. Someone had to take care of the situation, and I had to leave.'

Sara slid off the bed and simply looked at him, for once not bothered about her nudity. 'You're amazing, Guido.' She shook her head. 'When we met again you were convinced that I had suffered no more than a broken arm and bruising after losing the baby from my fall, and that I had lied to you and to the doctor, to everyone, so I could eventually demand money from your father and go home. Now you are admitting you *know* your version of events wasn't strictly accurate. In this new version I was a little unbalanced following the miscarriage—a situation made worse by the fact Caterina was not very nice to me. So, though you accept I didn't threaten your father with my story, I was still "a bit hysterical" and so you told your father to take care of the situation.'

'*Dio mio*, I wish I had never mentioned Aldo—never opened this can of worms,' he grated, and sat up in bed, running a hand through his tousled hair.

'I'm glad you mentioned worms,' Sara shot back. 'Because that was exactly what you were. A slimy worm who let his father do his dirty work for him. You asked him to get rid of me, and he did. To be brutally frank by that time I could not get away fast enough. And before you even think of denying it remember when we met again. You actually told me if I had hung around longer you would have paid even more to get rid of me.'

'You actually believed I wanted rid of you?' he asked, his dark eyes narrowed intently on her flushed and furious face.

'Yes.'

He closed his eyes and she saw the color leach from his face. She didn't give a damn.

'You can close your eyes to the truth, but it won't make it go away. And now we have got that settled, I need a drink.' And she walked out, leaving him sitting on the bed.

From sheer bliss to sheer hell in ten minutes, Sara thought, pouring herself a whisky and downing it in one go. She slammed the glass down on the table, and gasped. The fiery spirit caught her throat and she began coughing, her eyes watering.

She felt two strong arms enfold her, a hand stroke up over her head, and her face was pressed against a hard, warm chest.

'Please, Sara, don't cry. I can't stand to see a woman cry.'

She pressed her hands against his chest and lifted her head. 'I am not crying,' she spluttered indignantly. 'I wouldn't cry over you if you were the last man on earth.' Her blue eyes flashed sparks. 'The whisky went down the wrong way, you damned great oaf.'

To her astonishment, Guido threw back his head and laughed out loud.

'What's so funny?' she demanded.

'You are, *cara*. You let fly at me with any derogatory name that comes to your mind without the slightest fear. Pig, swine, and now damned oaf. You really should watch your language. A lesser person might take offence.' He grinned.

'I don't call anybody else names,' she shot back, and pushed out of his arms to shake a furious finger at him. 'Only *you* drive me to curse.'

Guido's eyes rested on her. Her head was thrown back, her perfect breasts thrust upwards, her long legs planted firmly apart, She was totally naked and bristling with frustration. His breath caught in his chest. *Dio!* But she was exciting. The most vibrant, sexy woman, the most beautiful…and she was his. A surge of desire mingled with exaltation went through him.

'And you know why that is, Sara?' he responded, with supreme masculine confidence. 'Because I am the only man who enflames your senses to the point where you can't help yourself, and you have to strike back any way you can.'

She saw the triumph in his black eyes as they swept lazily over her, and suddenly she was aware of her naked state—whereas Guido had donned a robe. Plus he was right—damn him…which only infuriated her further.

'Since when did you become a psychiatrist?' She shook her head, the anger draining from her. 'Believe what you like—you usually do. I need the bathroom,' she said flatly, and, turning, walked into the bedroom, then the bathroom, and locked the door behind her.

Sara had run away, she knew. But after recognising she still loved the arrogant devil she felt too weak to argue with him. She was terrified of giving away how she really felt. She splashed cold water on her face, swept her hair back and, snagging the towelling robe from the back of the door, pulled it on. She picked up the blue negligee from the floor and crumpled it into a ball. The fancy lingerie had lost what little power of protection she had imagined it gave her...she had no defence left. She loved Guido, and if ever a man did not deserve her love it was him, she thought sadly as she returned to the bedroom.

Guido was standing in the centre of the room. 'I was just coming to find you.'

She grimaced. 'I'm hardly likely to get lost in this suite. I'm beginning to know the place as well as my own apartment.' She sniffed, and crossed to where she had left her overnight bag. She stuck the blue gown—the now damp blue gown—inside, and a thought struck her. Straightening up, she turned hard blue eyes on Guido. 'You didn't use protection—' she blurted. 'Before—in the bathroom.'

'It is of no importance any more.' He shrugged. 'You are on the pill.' He reached out a hand. 'Come to bed.'

'For health reasons it certainly is,' she flung back, ignoring his outstretched hand. Remembering Mai Kim, and Margot, and heaven knew how many more women who shared Guido's favours around the world, adding in all their other partners—it was a hell of a mix…

'I trust you, Sara.' He smiled. 'I know you haven't slept around.'

The gall of the man—the flaming arrogance. *He* trusted *her*… 'What about Peter?' she flashed back.

'What can I say?' He flung his hands wide in an expansive gesture. 'I met up with him the other week when I was in Hong Kong. He was never your lover.'

'You… You…' she spluttered, incandescent with rage. 'You had the nerve to *ask* him? How dare you?'

'No, I took him out for a drink. Saki can be very potent to the unwary. He offered the information very dejectedly when he reached the maudlin stage.' And Guido had the nerve to smile again.

'Bully for you. So you found out I have never had a lover since you.' In her temper she told him more than she wanted him to know, and that simply made her madder.

While Guido's smile grew broader at her revelation, some odd emotion squeezed his chest.

'But my problem is,' she drawled acidly, 'that
you can't say the same. I know all about Mai Kim
in Hong Kong, and your lawyer friend Margot in
New York, plus the model in Italy—courtesy of
Peter, as it happens. Obviously he has a penchant
for telling the truth after a few drinks. But add
together all your lovers and their partners—*you*
I would not trust an inch…' she declared bitterly.
'I value my health too much,' she added for good
measure, staring straight at him.

The transformation was incredible. His face
was so taut with barely controlled rage that Sara
feared for her safety, and the air between them
was strumming with tension.

'You dare to say that to me?' Guido snarled,
filled with an ice-cold anger that he had never
experienced before. That Sara could reel off a
list of his past lovers was bad enough, but that
she'd had sex with him believing he had a string
of other women in his bed at the same time was
an insult too far. He prided himself on being
monogamous for as long as a relationship

lasted, whatever the temptation. But worse—the fact that she actually didn't care about his supposed other lovers at all except for how it might affect her physical health so outraged him he had to curl his hands into fists at his sides to stop himself throttling her. As for her lack of trust in him…

The injustice of it filled him with fury, and he grasped her upper arms and hauled her hard against him. 'You dare to suggest that I am careless with my sexual health and yours?' He focused on her with a dark, sardonic anger that heightened the tension between them almost to breaking point. 'You actually believe I sleep with a host of women at the same time?'

'Yes. But I doubt there is much sleep involved,' Sara ground out mockingly.

One hand grasped her jaw, and as he tilted her head back his glittering eyes bored down into her. 'And yet you share my bed—so what the hell does that say about you?' he demanded with a sneer.

Sara sucked in a deep breath. He was the same arrogant, conceited swine he had always been. Daring to question her morals when he had none. 'I am what you made me—what you want when you happen to be in England. A business deal—no more no less. So cut out the outrage. It won't wash with me. I know you too well. My God, do you think I *like* parading through this hotel every weekend? Do you think I didn't see the look in the receptionist's eyes when I booked in tonight?' she tossed back.

'In fact I am amazed that security here have not stopped me before now to question my morals—just like you. Next you will be trying to tell me you never had sex with Mai Kim and the rest…' She saw the subtle change in his dark eyes from rage to wariness, and a contemptuous smile twisted her lips. 'The way you keep calling me sweetheart is a dead giveaway—the typical ploy of a man who has trouble recalling the names of all his women at the relevant time. So don't make me laugh…'

'I have never felt less like laughing in my life.' He looked deep into her eyes and subtly the atmosphere changed. She was right about the sleaziness of their meeting in the hotel, and he was disgusted with himself for putting her in such a position. He also realised Sara was the only woman he had ever called sweetheart—a throwback to when they'd first met, because then, when his English had not been so perfect, he had meant it quite literally. Sara had had a sweet heart—a sweet innocence that he had adored—but he could not tell her that now. And the unpalatable thought crossed his mind that perhaps he was partially responsible for the cynicism she sometimes displayed.

'As for the rest,' he murmured, dismissing the disturbing thoughts from his mind. He lifted a finger and traced the line of her jaw, the outline of her lips, and slid his other hand down to close firmly around her waist and draw her to him. 'I can't deny I have known other women, Sara, but I *can* say—contrary to what your friend Wells and the press like to think—I have never had more than one lover at a time. From the moment we met again I have had no other lover but you. I want no other lover but you.'

Guido spoke with such conviction that Sara

wanted to believe him. She saw the desire in his darkening eyes, felt it in the hard length of his body pressed against her as his mouth took hers. It didn't matter whether she believed him or not. His kiss was enough to ignite the incredible hunger, the need she felt in the depths of her being for this man.

She shuddered when he lifted his head and slid his hand inside the lapels of her robe to cup her breast.

The scent of him filled her nostrils, the taste of him was like a drug—and she was totally addicted. Involuntarily she wrapped her arms around his neck, holding him close.

Guido stared down at her, his black eyes raking over her flushed face, the open invitation in her incredible eyes, and then lower, to where he fondled her lush breast. She was so hot, so receptive—and yet she didn't trust him. Why was that bothering him? And why had he told her the truth when he could have let her continue to believe he kept a string of women and given himself licence to bed any number of others? Any man's fantasy—except his. He groaned as she squirmed against him and shockingly realised *his* fantasy was to have the woman in his arms solely, totally his. He took her mouth once more…

CHAPTER TEN

GUIDO reached for his wristwatch, glancing at the time, then back to Sara, lying in the curve of his arm. A wry grimace twisted his firm lips. Amazingly he still wanted her, after having made love to her until almost dawn. Slowly removing his arm from her sleeping form, he rolled off the bed. Unfortunately it was after nine, and he had an appointment at ten-thirty. Willing his erection to subside, he headed for the shower.

Sara was still sleeping when, after he'd showered, shaved and dressed, he exited the bedroom. He called Room Service to order coffee and croissants, and logged on to his laptop. He flicked through the messages, answering some and ignoring others until Room Service arrived.

Sara awoke to a rattling sound and the strong smell of coffee. Guido was standing by a trolley, filling a cup with coffee. As she watched he placed a croissant on a plate and crossed to the bed.

He was fully dressed in natural linen pants and an open-necked shirt. His hair was still wet from the shower, and he looked incredibly fit and virile. Her lips parted in a slow, languorous smile. 'You're up early.'

'Not at all—it is nine-thirty.' He put the plate on the bedside table and held out the cup. 'Drink this, and eat. Then get dressed and packed. I want to be out of here by ten—hopefully never to return,' he said, with a dismissive glance around the room.

She took the coffee cup from his outstretched hand, lowering her eyes from his cool gaze, and took a deep swallow in an attempt to alleviate the sudden excruciating pain squeezing her heart. He was terminating their deal with the same ruthless efficiency with which he did everything. Obviously after their argument last night and the marathon sex session that had followed Guido had had enough of her, and he wanted her packed and gone. The irony did not escape her. As soon as she recognised she still loved him he was tired of her. Maybe he had sensed her need in the wild, abandoned passion of the night?

But, even knowing it was over, Sara couldn't help herself.

'What's the rush?' she asked weakly.

'We have an appointment at ten-thirty in Mayfair. So get a move on, woman.' He grinned and, turning back to the trolley, filled another cup with coffee, balancing a croissant on the saucer before heading for the door and throwing over his shoulder, 'I have a few calls to make, but don't be long.'

The relief Sara felt at that *we*—he was taking her with him—was out of all proportion, considering their deal. But she didn't question her feelings too closely. She simply drained her coffee and ate the croissant on the way to the bathroom.

Washed and packed, she slipped on the dress she had arrived in last night. It was either that or a pair of old jeans and a tee shirt that somehow she did not think quite appropriate for a meeting in Mayfair. Twenty minutes later she walked into the sitting room.

Guido glanced up from his computer, his arrested gaze fixed on Sara. A ray of sunlight highlighted the perfection of her features and turned her long silken hair to bronze. He snapped his computer shut and, like a man in a trance, walked towards her. She simply took his breath away.

She was wearing a pale yellow creation. Narrow straps curved over her slender shoulders to support the low-cut bodice revealing the soft curves of her breasts. Below her breasts was a band of white clinging material that accentuated her small waist and ended at her hips. A soft lemon skirt swayed flirtatiously a few inches above her knees.

'I love y-your dress,' he said huskily. 'You look good enough to eat.' And, curling his hands around her bare arms, he drew her towards him and dropped a swift kiss on her brow. He would have liked to do a lot more, but there wasn't time.

'It's the dress I arrived in last night,' she responded, slightly breathless—much to Guido's satisfaction.

'Mmm…nice. No man could resist you, looking like that. But resist you I must, or we will be late.'

Sara watched Guido escort the estate agent to the door. The woman was almost melting at his feet. She knew the feeling, and looked away to glance once more around the room. The floor was hardwood, and the ceiling had to be at least twenty feet high. It was minimally furnished, with three huge cream hide sofas grouped to face the wall of glass that was a window opening onto a huge terrace. The terrace was arranged like a Japanese garden, complete with a water feature, and the view over London was breathtaking.

The whole penthouse apartment—all ten rooms of it—was spectacular. Three bedrooms, three bathrooms, a dining room, living room, study and kitchen. Even the entrance hall was the size of Sara's living room. A bronze sculpture by the door discreetly housed the computer that operated just about everything in the place, from the high-tech sound system wired throughout the apartment to the massive flatscreen TV that was cleverly hidden in the wall of the living room. From the state-of-the-art security system down to the drapes at the windows—all controlled by a monitor in every room.

'So, do you like it?' Guido asked, slipping an arm casually around her waist.

She cast a sidelong glance up at him. 'I think it suits you.' The place had a stark but handsome appearance, and it was totally controlled— rather like Guido. 'But, yes—I like it.'

'Good—I'm glad you approve. It will make a perfect weekend retreat for us. No more hotels.'

'You didn't buy this just for that?' she exclaimed inanely.

'Not exactly.' He chuckled. 'As you know, I opened an office here some time ago, and I'd been thinking of buying a London base. Let's just say meeting you again gave me the added incentive to go ahead.' Turning her in his arms, he smiled down at her. 'What say we try out the bedrooms and see which we prefer?'

'I've only been out of bed a couple of hours.'

She was wary. A hotel was impersonal. With

her new awareness of her love for him she had a feeling sharing an apartment might very well be much more dangerous to her peace of mind.

'And, marvellous though this apartment is, I did notice the only food in the place is a gift pack on the kitchen table containing two bottles of champagne, a jar of caviar and some crackers. It's a beautiful day—why don't we take a walk around the area and see if we can find a grocery store.'

'The telephone usually works for me,' Guido said dryly. 'But if shopping is what you want to do—okay. So long as you realize—' he wriggled his black eyebrows up and down in an exaggerated gesture '—you will have to try out all three beds with me when we get back.'

'You, sir, are incorrigible.' But she could not suppress her laughter.

It was like a day out of time.

Guido took her hand in his as they walked along the pavement, and Sara was reminded of when they'd first met. Then they had wandered happily around the local area—not quite as up-market as this, but it had simply been about being in each other's company, sometimes stopping for a coffee or a drink.

She grinned up at Guido. 'You are not *really* going to take the doorman's advice and walk to Fortnum and Mason to get groceries?'

'The man said it was the nearest. And after that we are going to eat. Sandwiches last night and a croissant this morning is no diet for a man my size. Plus I need to build up my strength for later.'

They strolled past the Ritz and eventually reached Fortnum and Mason. Guido amazed her with his enthusiasm for shopping. She gave a wry smile when he said he'd never known shopping could be such fun. Given he had picked up all sorts of very expensive foods and wine that one would never find in a supermarket, she wasn't surprised. Nor was she surprised when at the end he simply ordered the purchases to be delivered that evening.

They meandered along Old Bond Street and he insisted on buying her a dress she admired in a designer shop window, along with a couple of skirts, trousers and casual tops—though the prices were anything but casual. She tried to object, but he overruled her with a smile and a reminder that it had been her idea to go shopping.

Finally they found a small Italian restaurant. Guido ushered her inside with a flourish, and, handing the designer carriers to the proprietor, entered into a quickfire conversation in Italian with the man as he led them to their table.

Seated at the table, Sara lifted sparkling eyes to Guido. 'What on earth did you say to him? The man bowed to me, for heaven's sake.'

Guido shrugged his broad shoulders, his expression bland. 'He was simply paying homage to your beauty and telling me how lucky I am.' And then he laughed.

Sara didn't know whether to believe him or not, but with his dark eyes gleaming into hers Guido was more relaxed than she could remember seeing him since the early days of their relationship, and she didn't care. They talked and laughed, and drank a bottle of red wine with their plates of pasta, and in Guido's case had steak to follow. They discussed the theatre, books, the world situation, and by unspoken mutual consent avoided any mention of the past. Guido even remarked that he had tickets for *Othello*—apparently the opera was opening at the end of October at Covent Garden, and a famous Italian singer was playing the lead role. Sara simply smiled.

Finally Guido, with the carriers in one hand and his other arm looped around her shoulders, led her back the way the way they had come. But not before stopping at a convenient pub for another glass of wine.

Sara could not remember the last time she had had so much fun, and when they finally returned to the apartment in the evening she told Guido so.

He took her in his arms, and was about to kiss her when the intercom sounded. Guido groaned and Sara, slightly tipsy, giggled when the doorman announced a delivery from Fortnum and Mason…

The delivery was still standing on the kitchen table where Guido had left it when the pair of them surfaced the next morning, having enthu-siastically tried out all three bedrooms…not to mention the huge wet room. They hadn't bothered with the steam. They'd generated more than enough between them…

Sara walked into the office late on Monday morning to face a huge bunch of roses, courtesy of Guido, on her desk. She blushed as red as the blooms at Jan's comments and questions. And as the week wore on it got worse. The meeting she had set up for Friday morning with Billy Johnson was attended by Guido, and he greeted her with a hug and a kiss, making no attempt to hide their relationship.

'Coffee, Sara.' Jan placed a cup on her desk. 'What are you so miserable about? You look like a woman who has found a pound and lost a hundred.'

Sara glanced up at her secretary. 'End of October, wet and windy weather, or maybe because I've put on a few pounds,' she quipped. 'Take your pick.'

'Hey, buck up. It *is* Friday—you have the whole weekend ahead of you with the gorgeous Guido. Yes?'

'Yes—you're right.' Sara smiled and took the opportunity to add, 'I'm leaving early today—about three.' She had a routine appointment with her doctor, to check on her first three months on the pill.

'I don't blame you. If I had a man like Guido I would want to spend hours preening and pampering before a date,' Jan said as she left the office.

If only everything was as simple as Jan thought, Sara sighed. But it wasn't, and never could be between her and Guido. Though lately she had allowed herself to dream…

Ever since Guido had acquired the apartment and insisted on giving her a key, their relationship had subtly altered from just sex to a much more conventional relationship—in her mind.

The roses sent to her at work, his turning up at her office supposedly on business, where he had made no attempt to disguise the fact they were more than friends by greeting her with a kiss in front of everyone…

She had remonstrated with him later, reminding him that theirs was not an ordinary affair, that he had blackmailed her into his bed. He had given her a sardonic look and said, 'So I paid for the pleasure? In my experience a man usually does pay for the woman in his life one way or another, be she his wife or his girlfriend, and I have no intention of slinking around hiding our affair from anyone. Get used to it.'

His cynicism had appalled her, but when he'd drawn her into his arms and kissed her she had made no argument.

The following Friday he had arrived at her apartment just as she'd got back from work. She had been reluctant to let him in to her own home, but he had looked so boyish, so pleased with himself, she had not had the heart to say no. Apparently he had taken delivery of a new sports car earlier that afternoon—a car to keep in London—and he'd wanted to give it a run.

Then there had been the mid-week phone calls he had taken to making from wherever he happened to be in the world, when they talked about anything and nothing, and on Guido's part sex—or the lack of it—because she was not with him…

Somehow over the past two months he had

subtly managed to infiltrate her everyday life, and if she was honest she rather liked it. True, the teasing from her office staff was embarrassing, and she hated to imagine what it would be like when they parted and she had to endure their sympathy. Because part they would—of that there was no doubt. But in the meantime she was doing exactly what Guido had said—living for the here and now and enjoying herself…and him…

Though sometimes, like this morning, when she woke up feeling sick, the shadow of their year-long deal hung over her like a dark cloud.

It was there buried deep inside her when they talked, walked or went out to the theatre, or shared a candlelit dinner in some exclusive restaurant. It was there when they simply sat in the apartment and watched TV or a film. And when he made love to her with savage, hungry passion, or gently with exquisite skill and tenderness, it kept the words of love that she ached to say locked in her heart. But Jan was right. Although the parameters of their relationship excluded any talk of the past or future, she was a lucky lady to have Guido for a lover…

On that happier thought, Sara drained her coffee cup and, lifting a file from her in-tray, concentrated on work. She had a sandwich for lunch at her desk, and by the time she left the office at three had completed a full day's work.

Two hours later Sara walked out of the doctor's office in a state of numb disbelief. She walked home in a daze, flopped down on the sofa and closed her eyes. It was incredible, unbelievable, but irrevocably true.

She was pregnant.

The doctor had asked if she had noticed any side effects from taking the pill, and she had told him she had gained a few pounds, and had felt a little nauseous lately, but other than that nothing. Then he had examined her. When he had told her she was pregnant—about two months—Sara had laughed disbelievingly. It wasn't possible. True, she had missed her period, but had put that down to having just gone on the pill. Calmly the doctor had asked if she could possibly have missed a pill, or been sick while taking it, which would have interrupted her protection. Then it had hit her like a thunderbolt…

How could she have been so dumb? After Peter had left for Hong Kong she had stopped taking the pill, berating herself for being stupid enough to start in the first place. Then, when she met Guido again, he had asked her if she was on the pill and she had lied simply to score a point—though she had started taking it again the following day. But at the time she hadn't planned on sleeping with Guido, and so hadn't thought about it in terms of contraceptive.

She could not believe what an idiot she had been. Guido…Guido— She leapt to her feet. She was supposed to be at his apartment by six.

She let herself in with the key.

'Where the hell have you been? I have been calling you for the last hour.' Immaculately dressed in a black evening suit, he was pacing the floor like a caged tiger. 'I expected you here when I arrived. In case you've forgotten we are going to the opera, and it starts in thirty minutes.'

'Sorry—I was with a client and switched my phone off,' she lied.

'Yes, well...' He strode over to her and, catching her shoulders, pulled her hard against him, claiming her mouth with his own in a deep, punishing kiss. 'Hell, you hardly have time to change—never mind anything else,' he growled in frustration. She knew exactly what he meant, but for once Sara was glad of the reprieve.

She could not deal with Guido now. She was in shock.

They got to Covent Garden with minutes to spare and were shown to their seats. Guido took her hand in his and she let him, for once barely conscious of his powerful presence at her side.

All she could think of was that she was having a baby. Since the moment she had miscarried the first time she had longed for another child. Only last year she had seriously thought of following in her mother's footsteps and opting for an unknown donor. And now she was pregnant.

Blindly she followed Guido to the bar in the interval, where she refused champagne—opting instead for sparkling water. By the time the opera was over she had a headache. She hadn't eaten all day, apart from a sandwich, and immediately she thought of the baby. Nothing and no one was going to prevent her having this child, she silently vowed.

Guido, with a hand at her elbow, led her out to the car, opened the passenger door for her, and then walked around to slide into the driving seat. But he didn't start the car. 'Are you going to tell me what is wrong, Sara?' he asked, shooting her a sidelong glance.

She looked at him then, taking in the scowl on his face. 'Nothing,' she murmured.

'Don't give me that. You have barely said a word all night. As for the opera—Othello could have murdered the whole cast as well as his wife and you wouldn't have noticed,' he said scathingly, and started the car.

Ten minutes later he stopped the car outside an exclusive restaurant. 'We have reservations for dinner. You do still want to eat, I presume?' he asked, shooting her an enquiring glance.

'Yes. Yes—of course.' Food was what she needed.

'Well, well—some enthusiasm at last,' he

mocked as he led her into the restaurant and helped her out of her coat.

Walking through the restaurant to their table, Sara was horribly self-conscious. She was aware of the tension in Guido as he walked beside her, resting a proprietorial hand on her waist, but she was even more aware of the interested glances from the customers—most of them women—directed at Guido. They were probably wondering what he was doing with a woman like her when he could take his pick from the very best, and frequently had in the past...

She had dressed in a panic, and she felt the black scoop-necked jumper dress was a bit on the tight side, a bit on the short side, and the black stilettos she had foolishly chosen accentuated the fact

She had done nothing with her hair but brush it straight back, and she was without jewellry or make-up, apart from lipstick which must have long since worn off. She glanced around the sophisticated and glamorous clientele of the restaurant and almost groaned. But instead she said, as the *maître d'* held out her chair, 'Excuse me—I need the powder room.'

She looked at her face in the mirror and grimaced. Then she looked in her bag. A lipstick and a sample mascara was all she had. She applied both and, feeling marginally better, made her way back to the table.

She felt Guido's eyes on her every step of the way, and he rose to his feet as she approached, his dark eyes roaming from her head to her toe and back again to narrow intently on her face.

'You look beautiful—as always,' he drawled, and for a wild moment she wondered if he had sensed her discomfort and was trying to reassure her. No, Guido wasn't the sensitive type, she thought as he stepped back and held out the chair for her.

Gratefully she sank into it, picked a bread roll out of the basket and began to eat. She felt Guido's eyes resting on her and looked across at him. 'I'm hungry. I only had a sandwich at my desk for lunch, and unlike you Italians I like my dinner no later than eight,' she said waspishly.

His mouth tightened. 'In that case I will order immediately.' And at a flick of his eyebrow, the waiter appeared.

She had upset him, and she didn't care. She had more to worry about than Guido's feelings or lack of them.

The food was excellent. Sara ate home-made soup followed by wild salmon in a delicious sauce, and ended with something light and sweet—unlike the atmosphere. She refused Guido's offer of wine, and had difficulty in concentrating on anything he said. The fact she was pregnant occupied her every thought. Her emotions fluctuated between elation and outright terror when she thought of the child she had lost. But with the terror came a steely determination to make sure nothing and no one prevented the safe delivery of this baby. She munched her way through all three courses because she had to. She was doing it for the baby.

'Whatever else is wrong, you certainly have not lost your appetite,' Guido remarked sardonically.

Sara glanced across at him, and the dark eyes that met hers held a gleam of barely leashed annoyance. 'I was hungry.'

'So I noticed. I trust your appetite will be

equally as voracious when we get home,' he drawled hardily. 'Now, let's get out of here.'

Sara made no comment, and stood up.

He paid the bill, helped her on with her coat and led her out to the car. Twenty minutes later, having parked the car in the underground car park of the apartment building, they entered the elevator. He leant back against the wall, every atom of his being focused on Sara's beautiful if somewhat washed-out face.

'Are you going to tell me what the silent treatment is all about?'

'Sorry,' she murmured, trying to placate him. 'I'm not feeling too great.'

'You do look rather pale,' he opined as the elevator doors opened.

'Actually, I have a splitting headache.' She told him the truth as he ushered her into the apartment and removed her coat before dropping it on a hall chair.

He reached for her again. 'The age-old excuse, Sara?' he queried sardonically, his hands resting on her shoulders. 'Or fact?'

'Fact. I'm not a great lover of opera. I do appreciate quite a few of the overtures and arias, but a whole performance is a bit much…'

'You should have said when I asked you.'

'I don't remember you asking,' she said, and he grimaced.

'Sorry. I am being a boor.' He drew her gently into the warmth of his big body, his arms wrapping around her. 'Mainly because you were not here waiting for me earlier.' A wry smile twisted his lips. 'But frustration will do that to a man. I am not cut out to be celibate and five days without sex is hard.' Bending his head, he brushed his lips lightly against her own. 'Come and sit down, and I will make you one of your disgusting cups of tea.' Having settled her on a sofa he loosened his tie and shirt as he headed for the kitchen.

CHAPTER ELEVEN

SARA kicked off her shoes, let her head fall back against the soft cushions and closed her eyes. It had been one hell of a day—but also, she thought, a slow warmth unfurling through every cell of her body, one of the best of her life. She was pregnant… She was going to be a mother…

She laid a hand on her flat stomach and took a deep breath. As for the father—she would have to tell him. She wouldn't deny Guido knowledge of his child. But this was *her* child first and foremost, and she was going to protect her baby with every breath in her body…

'Tea.' She opened her eyes to find Guido standing over her, holding out a mug of tea and two painkillers. 'Take these—they will help.'

She took the tea from his hand. 'Thank you,

but the tablets aren't necessary,' she murmured, and took a sip of the reviving brew.

'You are sure?' he asked, his dark eyes searching her pale face. 'You still look a little pale.'

'Positive.' She watched as he shrugged and crossed to the bar. He filled a glass with whisky, then strolled back to sink down on the sofa beside her.

'You are feeling better?' he asked, resting an arm around her shoulders. Raising his glass to his lips, he took a long swallow.

'A little.'

'Good.' He drained his glass and put it down on the table. 'In that case...' A slow, sensual smile curved his lips as he turned back towards her.

'I don't feel that well,' Sara quickly responded, even though the warmth of his hand on her shoulder and the close proximity of his body was doing alarming things to her pulse-rate.

'Then if not tonight...' he bent his head and brushed her lips lightly with his '...the morning is a certainty, which is a relief. There is not a lot of point in a weekend affair if half of it is without sex,' he said with a wry grin.

Whether he was teasing or not, Sara did not care. It was enough in her emotional state that he had said it. He had simply underlined what she had always known: he only wanted her for sex. And it made it a lot easier for her to say what she had to.

'I wouldn't count on that. I might be sick in the morning.' She tilted her chin to look up at Guido. A muscle was pulsing in his jaw, his mouth was a grim line, and she knew she had angered him but she didn't care. He was going to be a heck of a lot more angry when she told him her news. 'I'm pregnant…'

'You're what?' Guido demanded, his hand tightening on her shoulder. For a second he felt a surge of something very like elation, but it quickly turned to fury as he looked into her defiant blue eyes.

'You heard. I'm pregnant.'

For one blinding moment he wanted to strangle her. This was the woman who had caught him once before in precisely the same way. He leapt to his feet, picked up his glass and returned to the bar. He refilled it with whisky and downed it in one go. Sara had made a fool of him once. No one got away with that a second time. By an extreme effort of will he managed to control his temper. Only then did he slowly turn to lean back against the bar and let his gaze slide over her.

'So you say you are pregnant. Since when?' he demanded icily.

'The doctor estimates about two months.'

'How convenient for you. That puts me in the frame as the father, and yet you told me you were on the pill?' he drawled contemptuously. Did she take him for a complete idiot? He saw the tension in her slender shoulders, the slight flush of pink that covered her cheeks, and wondered what lies she would come up with this time.

'Yes, well…about the pill… I *was* on the pill, but I stopped taking it when Peter Wells left, and I started again after you and I—' She blushed even redder. 'I didn't want you to think I was the same innocent you first knew. Stupid of me, I know.'

She glanced at him slightly warily from beneath the thick curl of her lashes. She had a damn good *right* to be wary, trying to pull the same trick on him a second time, he thought.

'But according to the doctor—well, missing even one day can mean the difference between safe and unsafe.'

'So you're telling me what, exactly?' He strode towards her and, reaching for her upper arms, hauled her to her feet. 'That you are pregnant and the child is mine?' he snarled.

He could not credit what a fool he had been. All the signs had been there. Her refusal of champagne at the opera, her refusal of wine with dinner, her silence. Her refusal of the pain-killers. She had been setting him up for just this revelation but he was not stupid enough to believe her without proof.

'So when did you make this remarkable discovery?' he demanded through clenched teeth as he struggled to maintain a level of calm.

Sara swallowed hard. Held in a death-like grip, Guido's eyes boring down into hers, she felt afraid. But the thought of her baby gave her strength. Once he had intimidated her, but not any more.

'This afternoon. I had a three month check-up with the doctor to see how I was getting on with the pill, only to discover I was not,' she said bluntly. 'And it still wouldn't have made any difference if you had been more careful, if you recall the last night we spent in the hotel, and our rather hasty coupling in the bathroom. It does take two.'

'You bitch. You conniving, devious bitch,' he snarled, almost flinging her away from him.

Sara sank back down on the sofa and watched as Guido paced the length of the room, then flung open the glass doors and stormed out onto the terrace.

She felt the rush of cool air, saw him standing, tension in every line of his long body, and watched him lift a hand to rub the back of his neck. He looked like the most furious and frustrated man on earth, and in a way she didn't blame him. But in another way she was glad. Obviously he was horrified by her pregnancy, and that would make things much easier for her.

Rising to her feet, she slipped her shoes on, picked up her bag, and was walking towards the door when Guido's voice stopped her.

'Where the hell do you think you are going?'

Turning, she lifted cool blue eyes to his. 'I have told you I'm pregnant with your child. Whether you believe me or not is of no importance to me. I simply thought you had the right to know.'

'Don't take me for a fool, Sara. If this child is mine I will marry you again. But this time I am insisting on a DNA test. According to you, the night our child was conceived was the same night that you told me you didn't trust me. Well, I sure as hell don't trust *you*, and we will wait to marry until after the child is safely delivered.'

Sara shook her head. 'You, Guido, are incredible. I would *never* marry you again—been there, done that, got the tee shirt. Is that plain enough for you?'

'If you think for one moment I am going to fork out money to keep you and the child in luxury for the next twenty-odd years forget it. Marriage or nothing.'

'Great. Nothing suits me just fine. I wouldn't take a penny of your money. I am perfectly capable of looking after myself and my baby. Now I am going to call a cab and go home.'

She could not face him another second. Her emotions were threatening to overcome her. She felt like crying—why, she had no idea. Guido had behaved pretty much as she expected. He was furious that she was pregnant, and appalled at the prospect of being a father. And mad as hell that it might cost him money...

'Oh, no, lady—you are not walking out on me again,' Guido snarled, and, catching her by the shoulders, he looked grimly down into her defiant face. He had spent five minutes out on the terrace, trying to get his rage under control—to think straight and decide on a sensible course of action after her unexpected bombshell. That she had had the nerve to turn down his offer of marriage—admittedly an offer with conditions, but totally reasonable in his mind, given their past—so outraged him he felt like shaking her until her bones rattled.

'You and I have a deal. One year. And by my calculations you owe me nine months. You are not going anywhere.'

He was within a hair's breadth of losing his temper with her completely. He wrapped his arms around her and slid a hand up her back to twist in her long silken hair, before pulling back her head and taking her lush, deceitful mouth with his own. He kissed her with all the savage, angry passion roaring though him. He felt her initial resistance in some sane part of him and realised what he was doing, but he could not stop. Then he felt her catch fire, as always, and somehow it deflated his rage.

'We need to talk this through, Sara,' he murmured against her mouth, and gently stroked her back. He looked into her stunned blue eyes, saw the strain etched into her delicate features as she fought to control the emotions she could not hide, and smiled regretfully. 'Come to bed, and we will work something out in the morning.'

Breathless from Guido's kiss, Sara stared into his night-black eyes. *Work something* out, her brain finally registered. Was he for real? Late-night stubble roughened his square chin and outlined his sexy mouth, and he was smiling... Smiling...

Sara had nothing to smile about. She had

melted under the overpowering passion of his kiss like a snowflake in hell. And hell was what her life would be if she stayed with Guido. She snatched up her bag from where she had dropped it on the sofa. 'You have to be kidding.'

'Sara—' He made to reach for her again, but she swiftly sidestepped his hand.

'I've told you I'm pregnant. Duty done. As for your precious deal—forget it. Because I have. I know Dave and Pat already have the money. You can do your damnedest. I doubt they'll be able to hand the cash back over. I'm going home.'

She had to get out of here. She could feel stupid, angry tears burning at the backs of her eyes now, and it would be the final humiliation if she burst into tears in front of Guido.

She could remember all too well the last time she had really cried in his presence. It had been one of the worst nights of her life, and one that had effectively ruled out any future for her with him. However much she loved him—and she knew in her heart that she did and always would—her love for him could never override her deep-rooted fear of trusting him ever again…

'Don't be ridiculous,' Guido snapped derisively. 'You will never get a cab at this hour.' His great body tensed with rigidly controlled anger. He should have expected Sara to renege on their deal. He should have made her sign a contract. In every other area of his life he was one hundred per cent efficient, yet this blue-eyed she-devil managed to make a fool of him every time. Well, not this time.

Actually, Sara was wrong. The contract he had signed with Pat and Dave allowed for payments on a three-month basis, and contained an opt-out clause. But he saw no reason to enlighten her. It was enough to know that Sara, in spite of her beauty and her sexual charms, was still the same devious, money-hungry little witch beneath. She could not help herself, and he was no longer interested.

'I've had too much to drink to drive,' he said flatly. 'You will stay here tonight.'

'No…'

Her head lifted, her eyes betraying her dilemma. He saw the lingering sensuality in their blue depths—and surprisingly a flicker of fear. She wanted to do as he said. He could see it in the weary droop of her shoulders. She was exhausted and she was also pregnant. But obviously afraid he might make sexual demands on her.

'Don't worry—tired, pregnant women have never appealed to me. I will sleep in a guest bedroom,' he drawled sardonically. 'And tomorrow you can go where the hell you like. It's over…'

Sara decided to stay the night. There was not much point in storming off at two in the morning. She would wait ages for a cab. She walked into the master bedroom, oddly fearful, but there was no sign of Guido. She washed and, donning a baggy tee shirt, crawled into the king-sized bed, her mind spinning like a whirlpool.

Their argument was swirling in her mind. She wasn't actually clear on where Guido stood. He had gone from the most insulting marriage proposal to insisting she see out their twelve-month deal to declaring it was over.

Guido's last comment had been very final, and he had offered to sleep in the guest room all too readily. She remembered well the weeks before she'd miscarried their child the last time. Guido had barely touched her, put off by her growing belly and her sickness. This time he had shown his distaste straight away. No surprise there, then. She tried to tell herself she was pleased. But it was hours before she fell asleep.

She awoke the next morning and for a moment expected to see Guido in the bed beside her. Then the events of last night came flooding back and her stomach churned. Quickly she got out of bed and dashed to the bathroom, where she was predictably sick. She was standing under the shower, feeling almost normal, when the bathroom door opened. She saw the outline of Guido through the glass.

'What do you want?' she demanded.

The shower door was flung open. The water was turned off, and Guido was staring down at her, his eyes hard. 'I heard you being sick, and you have been in here long enough.'

She crossed her arms across her chest before realising the futility of the gesture. He had seen her naked countless times. Brushing past him, she snagged a towel from the rail and wrapped it around her body.

'Thank you for your concern, but it is not necessary.' He looked devastatingly handsome. His black hair was slicked back and he was wearing a grey cashmere sweater and black pants. Her stupid heart missed a beat—until she noted the cold, remote expression on his hard face.

'I am leaving for Italy in a couple of hours. Get dressed and I will take you home.'

'There is no need. I can get a cab,' she shot back.

'I've made you tea. Hurry up—I have no more time to waste.' His dark eyes flicked insolently over her. 'And I want to make sure you leave,' he declared bluntly as he walked away.

That last look said everything. It was as if she didn't exist except as a minor inconvenience in his busy life. Swiftly drying her trembling body, Sara pulled a bra and briefs from a drawer and slipped them on. She opened the wardrobe and eyed the assortment of clothes she had collected over the past few weeks. She picked out only the ones that were her own and left the things Guido had purchased. Donning an old pair of jeans and a sweater, she stuffed the rest in a holdall. She didn't bother with make-up and, tying her hair back in a ponytail, she picked up her bag. She took one last look around the room. She would never see this room again. The affair was well and truly over. She told herself she was glad, and headed for the kitchen.

Guido was leaning against the bench, a cup of coffee in his hand. 'Your tea.' He indicated the cup. 'It might be a little cold.'

She picked up the cup without looking at him, and took a sip. 'No, it's fine.' She downed the lukewarm liquid and replaced the cup on the bench. 'Let's go.'

'Shouldn't you have something to eat, in your condition?'

Sara cast him a scathing glance. 'I will when I get home. I thought you were in a hurry.'

He picked up her holdall without a word, and they left the apartment. But not before Sara had made a production of dropping the key he had given her on the hall table. 'I'll leave the key here. I won't be needing it again, but no doubt your next woman will.'

The journey to Greenwich was swift and silent, and the tension in the close confines of the car grew with every mile. Sara heaved a huge sigh of relief when he finally stopped outside her apartment block. She had her hand on the door before he turned the engine off.

'Wait, Sara.' And she heard the click as he locked the doors.

Slowly she turned her head. He had reached an arm around the back of her seat and his other hand was on the dashboard. 'What for? We said all there was to say last night.' She looked bitterly up at him. 'Except goodbye.'

'Maybe so. But I want you to understand I meant every bit of what I said last night. If—'

'Forget the if,' Sara cut in furiously.

Trapped in the width of his arms, with his face only inches from hers, she should have been wary, but instead temper came to her aid. He was looking at her, all cool, autocratic male, and she had had enough.

'And what "bit" would that be, exactly?' she continued before he could respond. 'The bit where you demanded a DNA test? Or the bit where you said you had no intention of paying for twenty years? Or maybe the bit where you told me you would marry me? Forget it, Guido. I would not marry an insensitive, arrogant ass like you for all the money in the world. Though maybe you're referring to the bit where you threatened to see my friends broke if I didn't continue to sleep with you? Truly, the only bit that interested me was the bit where you said it was over. Now, open the door.'

At her vitriolic outburst Guido's eyes had narrowed to mere shards of light, and he took a deep, steadying breath, fighting to retain his usual monumental control. That she had the nerve to dismiss him was unbelievable. If anyone had the right to be furious it was him. She had played him for a fool for the last time. But somehow, seeing her all flushed and furious and—yes—frightened…

He hung on to his temper by a thread. He hated emotional outbursts. They were anathema to his self-disciplined restrained temperament. He remembered how emotionally distraught Sara had become in Italy the last time she had been pregnant, and he knew now was not the time to argue with her. Now was the time to leave her.

She had shocked him last night and he knew he had behaved badly. He needed time to get his head around the fact he was going to be a father. A weekend on his yacht looked very inviting. And then he was going to focus on business for a while—something he had rather neglected of late. As for Sara, he concluded arrogantly, she needed time to cool down and see sense. Money or marriage. Either way he was going to have to pay. Despite his initial outburst to the contrary, he really didn't doubt for a moment the child was his. But he wasn't about to tell Sara. Let her sweat it out for a few weeks, realise what she was missing…

'Maybe I was overly harsh, Sara—understandably under the circumstances. To have a woman tell you she is accidentally pregnant a couple of months into a relationship is one hell of a shock to any man. And to have the same woman tell you the same thing in the same circumstances a decade later is one hell of a coincidence, you have to admit,' he declared sardonically.

Sara was disconcerted by Guido admitting he might have been harsh. Then two seconds later she was infuriated as he reiterated his archaic belief that she was out to trap him. 'Oh, I see. Now you have had to time to think, you still mean what you said last night. Right, I understand. Now, open the damn door. I need the toilet.'

'This isn't over, Sara. If what you say is true at some point we will have to talk.' His arms locked around her as his dark head dipped, and the air caught in her throat as his warm breath brushed her cheek. 'In the meantime…something to remember me by,' he said in a deep, sexy drawl. She tried to press her hands against his chest, to wriggle away, but there was nowhere to go in the flash sports car.

She tried to bite his tongue. Holding her with ease, he repaid her in kind with his own teeth, and then with his tongue he soothed and tempted until she had no more desire to bite. Instead her lips parted, and she succumbed to the building passion of his kiss. When he finally lifted his head, she stared up at him with wild dazed eyes.

'Goodbye, Sara—for now.' He unlocked the car door and slid out of the driving seat. She was still in a sensual haze when he opened the passenger door.

She let him help her out of the car and carry her holdall to the entrance of her apartment. Only then did she manage to speak. 'This is far enough, Guido.'

'Yes.' He glanced at the watch on his wrist. 'I have to get going. Look after yourself. I'll be in touch.' He ignored the elevator and turned to the stairs.

'Don't bother,' she yelled after him as he raced down the stairs without looking back.

Guido leaving was for the best, Sara knew. She closed the door behind her, dropped her holdall in the small hallway and headed straight for the kitchen. She wasn't going to cry. She was going to make a nice *hot* cup of tea, and bacon sandwich. She needed to eat for her unborn baby, she told herself firmly. Her child was her top priority—her only priority. She boiled the kettle, made the tea and grilled two rashers of bacon, totally ignoring the tears rolling down her cheeks... Sara ate, and she drank, and then with grim determination picked up her holdall and headed for the bedroom to unpack her clothes.

She brushed an angry hand across her eyes. She was not going to cry over Guido Barberi... She was not... But finally she collapsed on the bed and, hugging the pillow, buried her face in the soft down and let the tears fall. She cried for the love she had never had and never could have... She cried for the mother she had lost. The mother whose support at this time in her life she ached for. She cried for the child she had lost... She cried until there were no more tears left and then fell into a deep, exhausted sleep.

Sara woke some hours later and looked around the room. Her bedroom... Her apartment... She laid a hand on her stomach. Her baby... Her life... The tears had been cathartic, and amazingly Sara felt a strong sense of peace and hope for the future... Her mother had chosen to have her, to raise her on her own with love and care, and despite the tragedy of her early death her mother had done a good job.

Sara silently vowed she would be a good mother to her child. The inner strength that had helped her get over losing her baby and her marriage, to build a good career and make herself financially comfortable in the process, would serve her well now. She would devote that same strength of will and purpose, with the addition of love, to caring for her child for the rest of her life.

As for Guido... Who needed him? Certainly not Sara.

CHAPTER TWELVE

BUT Sara found it wasn't that easy to dismiss Guido from her mind over the following few weeks. Even though on the Monday morning after Guido had left she had changed her cellphone number yet again—just in case he tried to call. She did not want to speak, see or think of him ever again…

In response to Jan's question as to how her weekend had gone, Sara had told her the affair was over, Guido was gone, and if by any chance he called the office she was permanently unavailable.

But Jan had not let up, saying what a marvellous man Guido was, and how she was making a big mistake, until finally Sara had snapped. She had called Jan into her office and, swearing her to secrecy, told her the whole unvarnished truth. Their previous marriage, his blackmail, her pregnancy—the lot. Jan had been horrified, and with a shockingly fast turn-about had said she'd always thought there was something sinister about Guido. No man got filthy rich by being nice. And for a man of his enormous wealth and incredible good looks to be dating a small-time accountant hadn't really made sense.

Sara smiled at the memory now, and the unintentional insult, and paused for a moment on the way out of the kitchen after having washed up the dinner dishes. Five weeks of sleepless nights and fraught days, tormented with thoughts of Guido's touch, his kiss, the powerful driving force of his magnificent body sheathed in hers. Yet somehow she had not thought of him since she had arrived home tonight...

Perhaps Jan showing her his picture last week in a magazine, with a gorgeous blonde on his arm at a ball in Monte Carlo, had finally made her see sense and started the healing process. He was a playboy, with the morals of an alley cat. Always had been and always would be.

Amazingly, she had prepared her dinner, eaten

her meal, showered and changed into her new pyjamas. Guido hadn't entered her thoughts for over three hours. She smiled again.

Her step was lighter as she crossed to the sofa, sat down and picked up the remote control for the television. Her heart told her sadly that she would never stop loving Guido, but her head was telling her she was slowly learning to live with it, to smile again, laugh again, and, yes, love again. She put a gentle hand on her stomach, and she felt the love...

Relaxing, she switched on the television. An advert for Christmas caught her attention and she realised the holiday was only three weeks away. Tomorrow she would go shopping, she decided, and—God willing—this time next year she would be shopping for her child. Feeling better than she had in ages, she flicked through the channels.

Friday night viewing. She had a choice between game shows, talk shows and an American murder mystery. She chose the murder mystery, and settled back to watch.

The doorbell rang and, clicking the remote to

mute, she rose to her feet and crossed to open the door. Jan had said she might pop round later. In fact Jan had been acting like a mother hen ever since Sara had told her she was pregnant.

She opened the door and stepped back, her mouth falling open, her eyes widening in disbelief. Because Guido was standing there. Tall and dark, he was silhouetted by the hall light, his face in shadow. Silent, unmoving, he looked down at her with an intensity she could feel to her soul.

Finally finding her voice, she said unevenly, 'Leave. You are not welcome in my home.' And she did what she should have done straight away—closed the door in his face. Or tried to. But a highly polished designer loafer stuck in the opening.

'Not so fast, Sara.' A broad shoulder shoved the door back and she watched helplessly as he walked past her and strode into the middle of her living room.

He was wearing a full-length black cashmere overcoat, and when he turned around she was stunned to see he was holding a bunch of red roses upside down at his side. Meanwhile she was still standing, numb with shock, holding on to the door handle. If she didn't Sara thought she might fall. Her legs had gone weak just at the sight of him. She raised astonished eyes to his face.

'You changed your number again, Sara,' he said curtly. 'And your secretary refused to let me speak to you today.' He gestured with the hand holding the flowers. 'What crazy game are you playing at now, woman?'

'Me? Playing…? You march into my home, wielding a bunch of roses like a baseball bat, and have the nerve to ask me that.' She let go of the door handle and walked towards him. '*You* are the only player around here—as the world press confirms with amazing regularity.' It was only as she got closer that she saw him clearly. His handsome face looked haggard, and his wickedly sinful eyes looked raw. For an instant her heart twisted inside her. Maybe he was ill…

No, Guido was never anything other than perfectly healthy, she thought bitterly. Not ten minutes ago she had been thinking she was beginning to get over him, and now here she was, back to square one. Her face felt warm, and other more intimate places were warming up simply from looking at him. But not for long, she swore. Though how she was going to throw him out presented a bit of a problem, she thought, casting another glance over his towering frame.

'You are to be the mother of my child. I have the right,' he said harshly, his voice rising. 'Did you really think I would let you cut me out of your life again?'

'My God, that is some turnaround.' Suddenly Sara was blazingly angry. 'I seem to remember you demanding a test before you would even consider you might be the father, and then telling me our relationship was over. Which is just fine by me. If suddenly you have decided differently, then tough. I don't want to know. You are not good father material. I remember all too well how useless you were the first time. And I learn from my mistakes.'

He gasped, and she saw the harsh stain of red across his high cheekbones, saw the anger in his eyes as he took a step towards her. She recoiled instinctively. But surprisingly he stopped, and in an instant he had himself under control again.

'I did not come to fight with you, Sara,' he said slowly. 'I came to apologise, for questioning that the child you're carrying is anything but mine. It was sheer temper on my part, and once I began to calm down I knew without a shadow of a doubt the child could only be mine.' He paused. 'And also to give you these.' He handed her the roses, and unthinkingly she took them.

'A romantic gesture suggested by my kid brother. Apparently sending flowers is not enough. Presenting them in person is the way to go. It works for his wife, he assured me. I thought it might work for me, but I should have had more sense than to listen. I have a feeling it is too little too late—and anyway I'm not the romantic type.'

'You've got that right,' Sara flashed back. 'In my experience the only gifts you give to a woman personally are of the skimpy lingerie variety—more for your own pleasure than hers,' she said bitingly.

His lips twisted. 'I never saw it that way, but

I can see how you might. I apologise if I offended you.'

'Offended?' she exclaimed. He'd done more than offend her. He'd blackmailed her into his bed, made her pregnant, made her love him all over again. She opened her mouth to tell him just what she thought of him. But he silenced her with a wave of his hand.

'Please, Sara—no argument. Not now. Just let me say what I have to say, then I will leave you in peace.'

Slowly it dawned on Sara that this was a Guido she had never seen before. Gone was his arrogance, his supreme confidence. He looked like a man on a mission he did not particularly like, and it worried her. What was he up to?

'If this is going to be a speech, I'm going to sit down.' And, suiting her actions to her words she walked past him and resumed her place on the sofa. 'Hang on a minute while I set the television to record. I was watching a rather good film when you so rudely interrupted,' she said prosaically.

The fact that he made no scathing remark,

simply shrugged off his overcoat and dropped it on the arm of the sofa opposite and sat down worried her even more. His hair was longer than she had seen it in years, and he was wearing denim jeans and a black roll-necked sweater. The kind of casual clothes he had worn when they'd first met.

He ran a distracted hand through his hair. 'Where to begin?' he murmured.

'At the beginning is a good start,' Sara said facetiously, and he looked at her then, his dark eyes capturing hers.

'You're right. When we first met I thought you were the most beautiful girl in the world...still do.' A wry smile curled his lips. 'Maybe we would have married anyway, but the fact you were pregnant decided it for of us. We both know what a disaster that turned out to be. But, contrary to what you think, I did grieve over the loss of our child. When I saw you in the hospital bed, all bruised and broken, I was gutted. And I felt so guilty. You were so young. You should have been enjoying your teenage years, enjoying university, and because of me you were hospitalised in a foreign country and had lost our child.'

'The past is irrelevant—' Sara began curtly. She wanted no post mortems. She just wanted him gone.

'No—let me finish.' He rose to his feet and crossed to the patio window to stare out over the river. 'I have to do this,' he said slowly, turning back and crossing to sit down beside her. He bent forward, his long legs splayed and his elbows resting on his knees as he clasped his hands between his thighs, not looking at Sara.

She moved slightly, not comfortable with him so close.

'I knew I had not given you the attention and the support you deserved as my wife. In my defence, the business was in a mess. I had tried to tell my father countless times what was needed, but he would not listen. So I went to London. When I returned with you as my bride the business was in an even worse state. He had let contacts slip, never visited our American associates, and he had no choice but to let me take over. I had to work extremely hard to modernise and build back customer confidence in the firm. It's no excuse, I know.'

He glanced at her then, his mouth twisting sardonically. 'I should have put you first, but I was obsessed with making a success of the firm. I was going to be a father, I was going to have a family to provide for, and I took you for granted. A vibrant, sexy, pregnant wife waiting at home. What more could a man want?'

'Really, Guido, there is no need for this. And there is no need for you to feel guilty.' That he had felt for the loss of their baby unsettled her more than she wanted to admit. She could just about get over him believing he was heartless. She did not want this softly spoken vulnerable Guido, because he pulled at her heartstrings in a way that frightened her. She made to get up.

'But there is.' He sat up and wrapped an arm around her shoulders, angling his big body towards her, and the look of raw pain in his dark eyes stunned her. 'I finally know the truth. Caterina *did* push you down the steps.'

After all the pain and suffering he had caused her for one vengeful moment Sara wanted to say, *So what? I told you so*. But she bit back the brutal comment as he continued.

'And, God help me, if she wasn't already dead I'd kill her. I know one should not speak ill of the dead, but I hope she rots in hell for what she did to you.'

His black eyes flared with such vitriol Sara believed him. He took a deep breath, as though to control the violence of his thoughts.

'I don't expect you to forgive me for not trusting your word, Sara… But perhaps over time we can put it behind us…' He paused. 'I know I have no defence for my lack of faith in you. But I simply could not envisage anyone being so evil, and, given your fragile state, I believed the doctor when he told me it was delusion and a result of your concussion.'

'Fragile state? Crazy, you mean…That's what you called me when we met again on the yacht. You called me a *crazy bitch*,' Sara tossed back at him. That still rankled. 'So what made you change your mind?' She was mad as hell. And not a little hot, with his hand squeezing her shoulder and his thigh hard against her own.

'What caused this sudden epiphany?' she demanded. 'Sure as hell nothing *I* said.' She could not believe Guido's arrogance. Even when he was asking for forgiveness he was planning his next move.

'My father told me.'

Her lips parted in shock. 'He knew... Then why did he—?' She never got the chance to finish the question as Guido cut in.

'Not at the time, Sara. He found out when he was informed of Caterina's car accident and dashed to the hospital to see her. She knew she was dying, and she confessed to him that she had pushed you and got the gardener to lie for her. Apparently they had been having a sexual affair for some time, and the man was happy to agree—along with taking a rather large sum of money to keep his mouth shut. But she did not want to die with it on her conscience.'

'Good for her,' Sara said flatly. 'But why did your father not tell you the truth before now?'

'You have to understand Caterina was his half-sister's child—his responsibility from the age of five, the only girl in the family. You, on the other hand, were my shotgun wife. He is an old-fashioned man to whom family is everything, and he did not approve of the circumstances of your birth. As you had already lost the child, and we had been divorced for years, he thought there was no point in besmirching Caterina's memory because she was family...' His voice was hard. 'You were right all along. He abhorred your lack of a father. With the exception of my mother and Aldo my family treated you abominably—criminally, even. And to my ever-lasting shame, I am so very sorry.'

She drew in a stunned breath. 'And he told all this because...?'

'Because I had a furious argument with him over lunch today, and he had no choice but to finally tell me the whole truth if he ever wanted to see me or any child I might have ever again. He had already admitted you never asked for money. What he left out in his previous confession was that he had demanded you take it and seek medical help in England or he would call the doctor and have you returned to the hospital. He also finally recalled that he knew Caterina had pushed you.' He paused. 'I can't begin to imagine how terrified you must have been. You were a young girl in a strange country and I blame myself totally.'

Sara wasn't ready to absolve him. He might be contrite, but it altered nothing. Though the pain and the shame in his black eyes made her heart squeeze in her chest.

His mouth twisted. 'I would still be in the dark if it wasn't for Aldo yet again,' he continued slowly. 'After I left you I intended spending the weekend on my yacht, but actually it was only a day.' He grimaced. 'I refused to take any crew with me and then the weather turned nasty. I had been drinking, and when I tried to return to the harbour I managed to hit the outer wall and wreck the prow of the yacht. I had to be towed in.'

Sara almost laughed at the look of self-disgust on his handsome face.

'Anyway, I returned to work, and in the last few weeks have probably circled the globe a couple of times—raising hell with all my staff, according to Aldo. When I stopped in Naples on Thursday he took me to task. A sobering experience in both meanings of the word. I told him I had got you pregnant again, and he told me I was an idiot for letting you go the first time, and an even bigger fool for walking away this time. Then he finally told me everything that had happened when he and Marta visited you in hospital. Seemingly you told them you didn't like the room you had been transferred to, and that the medicine you were being prescribed made you woozy. And Caterina had pushed you down the stairs. Unlike me, Aldo was inclined to believe you—and with the clarity of youth he pointed out that you were now in the psychiatric wing of the hospital and if you ever wanted to get out to tell the psychiatrist what he wanted to hear. That you had remembered everything and been mistaken about Caterina, probably because she was the last person you had seen when you left the house, and actually you had simply slipped.'

He flung back his head. 'When he told me, I couldn't believe it. I could not face the fact I had been so stupid. My kid brother knew my wife better than I did. He also told me that unless I wanted history to repeat itself I should get back to you as quickly as possible and beg your forgiveness. It was only when my father confirmed the truth today that I finally accepted what an arrogant, blind bastard I had been and took Aldo's advice.'

She stared at him. 'Is that why you are here? Because your brother told you to come? My God, you know how to insult a woman.'

'No—I came because I can't stay away.' He paused. 'In my arrogance I thought I could.' He gave a harsh laugh. 'When you told me you were pregnant a second time my immediate reaction was one of elation quickly followed by fury, my cynical mind rebelling at what I thought was a trap. I was so messed up I couldn't think straight. The next morning I actually thought I would leave you alone for a month or two, let you realise what you were missing, and then stride back into your life to accept your undying gratitude and love when I offered to marry you again.'

'That *is* arrogant,' Sara murmured and yet she felt herself begin to tremble.

'Over lunch today I told my father of my intention—hence the argument. In my father's defence, at the time you miscarried he genuinely believed the gardener's story, and he really did think you were ill. He did not want me tied to a mentally ill wife. Disgusting, I know, but from his point of view understandable.'

His long fingers squeezed her shoulder as though to emphasise his point as he moved closer, his taut dark face only inches from her own. 'I swear to you, Sara, I honestly thought you were confused because of losing our child. I was only twenty-four—knew nothing about women's problems. Still don't.' He looked almost as confused as Sara felt. 'I only thought badly of you when I returned from America and my own father lied to me, making you out to be a money-grabber. Then, when he confessed he had lied a couple of months ago, and Aldo made me face the fact Caterina had not treated you very well, I told you and apologized. I thought that was the end of it. How wrong I was. My own father was still withholding the truth from me.'

This new concerned and repentant Guido was

much more dangerous than the arrogant version, and Sara could feel herself weakening towards him. She could understand how betrayed he must feel by his father if what he said was true, and she was inclined to accept Guido's treatment of her years ago had been more out of ignorance than any bad intent.

'I rang the doctor before I left this afternoon.' His hand eased on her shoulder, his fingers stroking up the side of her neck, and she could feel her pulse start to race. 'He assured me even he was convinced you were genuinely ill. I could never have imagined in a million years Caterina could be so ruthless.'

'Yes, well, that is very interesting.' She tore her gaze away from his dark sombre eyes and leant forward, dislodging his hand from her shoulder. 'But it is all water under the bridge now.' She wriggled along the seat and got to her feet. 'I'd better put these flowers in water.'

Sara bent to reach for the flowers, but a long arm curved around her waist, hauling her back on the sofa. A large hand swooped down and flung the roses across the room.

'Damn it, Sara—is that all you have got to say? I am baring my soul here, begging your forgiveness, trying to tell you I love you, and you want to water the bloody roses.'

Her lips parted in shock. 'You what…?'

'You heard…I love you,' he flashed back, and the anger in his dark eyes was anything but loving. 'You think it is easy for me to admit I have been a complete and utter idiot for over a decade? I loved you from the moment I saw you. The first time I made love to you was the most incredible experience in my life. I thought I had died and gone to heaven. You were so exquisite, and when you told me you loved me I felt like the king of the universe. You were mine—all mine.'

The shock in her eyes softened as they met his, and her lips curved in a faint smile. 'You never said anything,' she reminded him.

'I was young and stupid—and, if I'm honest, scared. In my arrogance I told myself I was feeling so great simply because it was the best sex I had ever had. The fact that you loved me was all I needed to know.'

Sara's smile faded somewhat and she stirred restlessly. He tightened his arm around her back and, slipping his other hand beneath her legs, lifted her bodily onto his lap, cradling her against him.

'I was in love with you then, Sara.' His dark eyes bored into hers and she could not tear her gaze away. 'But I was too much of an emotional coward to tell you.'

Guido admitting he was a coward was unthinkable, but there was no doubting the genuine contrition in his dark gaze.

'When you said you were pregnant I couldn't wait to marry you. I told myself I was only doing it for the baby, but that was not true. I lied to myself. When we went to live in Italy I thought all I had to do to keep you happy was give you a spacious home and plenty of sex. I was so tied up in work I had no patience with you.'

'You mean you never listened to me.'

'Yes,' Guido admitted. 'I didn't want to hear of problems at home. I had enough at work. I have no excuse for what I did ten years ago, or for what I didn't do.' He gave a jerky shrug of one shoulder. 'I didn't take care of you and our baby as I should have done, and for that I will feel guilty to my dying day.'

She lowered her head, unable to stand the anguish in his eyes, but still not sure of his avowal of love. Miracles don't happen, she told herself. This might just be a ploy to get her baby.

His arm tightened around her back, and with his other hand he cupped her chin and gently lifted her face to his. 'I can only beg that you will forgive me in time and give me a another chance. Let me show you I can protect and care for you and our baby. Let me show you how much I love you.' His hand smoothed a few tendrils of hair from her cheek and she trembled.

She could see the love, the need and the vulnerability in his dark eyes. She was drowning in the warm, masculine scent of him and she was on the brink of melting. 'You love me…'

'I love you. Only you. If it is any consolation to you, it tore me apart when you left Italy. I told myself I didn't care, told myself I hated you—'

'I told myself the same,' Sara murmured.

'You had good cause then,' Guido said gruffly, frowning down at her. 'And before you say it I know you have even more cause now. When I saw you again on the yacht I was determined to have you. Retribution time, I thought, for the girl who walked out on me. I blackmailed you into sleeping with me and it backfired on me. Because I knew the morning we left the hotel for the last time that I loved you. I almost told you. Instead I chickened out and said I loved your yellow dress. For a while I thought everything was perfect, and then you said you were pregnant—and I walked out on you.' He cupped her cheek. 'Sara, I am totally ashamed of what I did, and I don't expect you to love me.' His face was grim. 'But I swear if you let me I will spend the rest of my life trying to atone for all the wrong I have done you, and hopefully in time you will find it in your heart to forgive me.'

His dark eyes shimmered fiercely over her lovely face, and she remembered the morning when she had thought for a moment he was leaving her, her relief when she grasped that he wasn't, and she recalled his comment on her dress.

He did love her. She moved slender hands into his black hair and drew his mouth down to hers.

'I forgive you. Kiss me.' She sighed. His mouth covered hers, and it was some minutes before she remembered to breathe again.

'Oh, God, Sara. It has been hell staying away from you,' he groaned, and somehow she was lying on the sofa, and Guido was removing his clothes and hers with more speed than skill. 'I want you so much.'

She let her hands roam down over him. 'I can tell,' she teased. She traced the curve of his lips, and just about everything else, with a tender delight that made him groan, and what followed was a wild, passionate and incredibly sensual loving.

Afterwards he told her again he loved her, in English. Sprawled on top of him, she licked the smooth, damp skin of his strong throat and he told her again in Italian. She sighed her delight and, crossing her arms across his broad chest, felt a deep well of tenderness surge inside her. Guido— her lover, her arrogant, conceited, confused, wonderful man—loved her, and she smiled.

Guido looked up into her sparkling blue eyes and couldn't believe his luck. He had been prepared for her to throw him out—had expected it once he'd learned just how badly he and his family had failed her. But beautiful, generous Sara—the woman of his dreams, his soul mate—had forgiven him. He didn't deserve it, but he was never, ever going to let her go again.

A broad grin split his darkly handsome face. 'So, when are you going to marry me?' He felt the tension snake through her relaxed body, and slowly it dawned on him that Sara, while accepting everything he had said, had never said she loved *him*. And from the evasive look in her blue eyes she was not about to marry him.

'Don't let's think about that now.' She rolled off him. 'I need a drink.'

Guido clenched his jaw and concentrated on keeping hold of his temper, forcing himself not to demand an explanation. He wanted her in every which way there was, bound to him by unbreakable bonds, but he knew he had to tread softly. He had trampled all over her before. He was damn lucky she was pregnant with his child and back in his arms. He could wait for the rest…marriage and her love…

Sara pulled on her pyjamas without looking at the magnificently naked male sprawled on her sofa. She had fallen into his arms, as usual. He'd said he loved her, and she actually believed him. He had shown her with every kiss and caress. But marriage…

'Make mine a coffee—black and plenty of sugar. I need the energy.'

She straightened and glanced at Guido. He was lounging back against the sofa—thankfully he had pulled his boxers back on—and a lazy smile played about his sensuous mouth.

She heaved an inward sigh of relief. The subject of marriage was forgotten—thank heaven. 'Certainly, sir.' She gave him a beaming smile and, unable to resist, bent over him and dropped a loving kiss on his lips.

Two strong hands grasped her waist and held her fast. She laughed down at him, but her laughter vanished as she saw the seriousness in his dark eyes.

'Why won't you marry me, Sara? I made a

terrible mistake, but you said you forgive me. I know you, Sara. You could not respond the way you do when we make love unless you felt something for me. So what is stopping you?'

'Once bitten twice shy,' she said lightly.

Standing upright, he wrapped an arm around her waist and laced one hand into the silken fall of her hair to tip her head back. 'This is not a joke,' he said fiercely. 'We are having a baby, Sara.'

'I know that. But does the blonde babe you had on your arm last week know, I wonder?' she shot back, using the memory of his picture in the magazine to divert him from her real reason.

'Ah—you are jealous.' And the look of relief on his face was almost comical. 'You saw the picture of me at the Monaco charity ball.' His fingers combed her hair back into a semblance of order. 'You have nothing to worry about, Sara. She was simply one of the models who was hired for the fashion show. I had never even met the woman before. She was in the line-up for the publicity shot, and happened to be next to me. I love you—only you.'

There was no doubting his sincerity in his

black eyes, the tenderness in the fingers that trailed from her brow to trace the delicate curve of her cheek, and desire curled in her stomach. Her breasts felt constrained beneath their velvet covering as her sensitive flesh swelled and her nipples peaked into tight, straining buds. She wound an arm around his neck and placed her other hand on his chest. She felt the heavy thud of his heart beneath her palm, and she trembled with the powerful force of the sensations roaring through her. Then he kissed her. A long, deep, tender meeting of mouths, a kiss like no other, with gentle passion and the promise of love.

When he lifted his head, she could not drag her eyes away from his.

'I will keep asking until you say yes, and finally love you into submission. Have you thought of that?' he teased, his throaty voice shaking slightly as she stared up at him.

She could deny him no longer. The love in her heart was expanding to fill every corner of her being. And she knew she had to tell him the truth. 'I might very well let you—because I *do* love you, Guido,' she murmured.

He crushed her in his arms. 'You love me? You really love me?' he demanded fiercely, and she nodded her head.

'Yes. But I don't want to marry you. I can't—I'm too afraid.'

'Afraid?' he husked, and held her close, sensing her distress. 'Why? Because of what happened before? I can't change the past, but Caterina is gone; there are no more dark secrets in my family. If you let me, I will chase all your fears away—I promise.'

'At least you *have* a family,' she said softly. 'When my mother died. I was put in a children's home at first, and I slept in a dormitory. My bed was beneath a window—a barred window. It was horrible. I was terrified of them. I hated looking up and seeing those bars, and on a clear night the shadow of the bars was bigger and even more terrifying.'

'*Mia cara*, my heart aches for you,' Guido murmured, and ran a soothing hand up her back.

'Yes, well…I had nightmares about them for years, until Lillian came into my life. By the time I went to university I was fine.' She looked up at him with huge solemn blue eyes. 'But when I was in the clinic in Italy the room they moved me to had bars. I had to lie to get out, and I took your father's cheque because he was going to call the doctor if I didn't and put me back in the clinic. I vowed then I would never give any man that kind of power over me ever again.'

'Oh, *Dio*, no,' Guido groaned.

'You understand now why I won't marry you?' She wriggled out of his hold and he let her. 'I would be quite happy to continue as we are.'

'But you don't trust me—and I don't blame you.' Distraught, Guido ran a hand through his hair. 'I'll do whatever you want.' He had continued to work all the hours under the sun after she'd miscarried and been in hospital, and then he had told his father to take care of her when he'd left for America. The full horror of what he had inadvertently subjected her to completely defeated him. It would haunt him for the rest of his life.

'In that case you can come and help me make the coffee.' A tentative smile curved her luscious lips, and Guido followed her like a lamb into the kitchen. But later that night he turned into a tiger in the bedroom.

'So where are we going to live?' Guido asked the next morning as they faced each other over the small breakfast table.

He had done some deep thinking during the night, while watching Sara sleep. He loved her, and she loved him. Eventually they would marry, he decided. But first he had to prove to her she could trust him.

'My apartment or yours?' He saw her pleased surprise and was heartened by it. He had never fully appreciated how devastating it must have been for Sara when she lost her mother. Or the horror of being in a home before she was fostered. Sara had told him about Lillian years ago, but he had never met her, and to be honest he had never really listened. His hormones had been raging, and all he'd thought of was sex at the time. On top of everything else Sara did not even know who her father was. It was up to him to allay all her fears, and the best way was to take it one step at a time.

'I can quite easily work from London, and you probably want to keep your job.'

'Yes. Oh, yes.' Sara danced around the table and flung her arms around his neck. 'Do you really mean you will live here with me?' She was astonished at how reasonable he was being.

'Well, my apartment in Mayfair is bigger, and has a study, but that is the general idea. After all, who needs to marry when they have a sex buddy like you?' He grinned.

'Okay, your apartment it is,' Sara said happily, and was swept up in a pair of strong arms and carried back to bed.

EPILOGUE

'I'VE never been to America before,' Sara said, stating the obvious, as she stared out of the hotel window at the New York skyline, at the myriad lights blinking and flashing, outlining the huge skyscrapers. She could actually identify the Empire State Building.

Guido walked up behind her, admiring her slender silhouette through the diaphanous fabric of the negligee she had slipped on. His body stirring, he looped an arm around her waist as he drew her back against him. 'So what do you think, Mrs Sara Barberi?'

Sara turned and looked up into his gleaming black eyes, her own sparkling like sapphires. 'I think it is fabulous and huge.' She laughed, and raised the glass of champagne in her hand. 'A bit like you, husband.'

Guido chuckled and clicked his glass against hers. 'To us—always.'

Curved in the crook of his arm sipping champagne, Sara concurred.

'Do you think Anna will be all right?' she asked as she drained her glass. 'We've never left her overnight before, and she is only four months old.'

Guido took the glass from her hand and placed it on the table with his. Catching her hand in his, he said, 'Stop worrying. She will be fine. Marta and Aldo will spoil her rotten. This is our wedding night, and I think we should get on with the honeymoon.'

Sara looked at him, her eyes full of love. 'I thought we already had.' She gestured to the massive bed behind them—the bed she had just left to look at the view, after being thoroughly loved by her husband.

'Okay, Sara—you're right. I've booked a table in the restaurant for dinner. I'll grab the shower first…or you could join me. Don't be long.'

Sara's eyes followed him. A white towel slung around his hips was his only covering, and his body gleamed bronze in the subdued lighting. He was magnificent, and he was hers.

The last ten months had been fantastic. They had moved in together, and baby Anna had been born in late May. Guido was a wonderful man, loving, generous and kind, and he absolutely doted on their little girl. He had chosen the name Anna Lily after Anne, the mother Sara still missed and Lillian, the woman who had been her honorary big sister and best friend when she'd needed one most. Sara had been incredibly moved by the gesture as Guido's acknowledgment of her past and a thank-you to the women who had loved her.

Last month they had flown to Italy, and she had finally faced Guido's father. It had not been half as bad as she'd expected. He was a frail old man, and hadn't been able to apologise enough for what had happened before. Marta and Aldo had visited them in England before the baby was born, and they were all firm friends. This morning the whole family had arrived in Greenwich for their wedding in the local church.

It had been a splendid service, with all her

friends from work, and Pat and Dave. Billy Johnson and his family had arrived in the new pleasure boat, and the wedding breakfast had been held in the restaurant on board while the boat cruised along the Thames. At two in the afternoon they had boarded a plane for America and arrived here, with the time change, at four. A drive through New York in a limousine, and they had been in their hotel suite by five-thirty. And they had been in bed for the last couple of hours. Sara sighed happily. Life could not get any better.

'Tired, sweetheart?' She felt the brush of his hand against her cheek and, turning her head, looked up at him. 'Or regretting you married me again already?'

Even now she could see the slight uncertainty in his dark eyes, and she knew she had put it there with her refusal to marry him sooner. She reached up and wrapped her arms around his neck. 'Never. It was a wonderful wedding, and I am only sorry I made you wait so long, Guido. I love you, and I trust you with my life.'

'Damn, I wish we weren't dining in the restaurant.'

'You could cancel,' she teased.

'Not this time,' he said with a grimace. 'Get dressed—and make it quick. The table's booked for eight-thirty.'

Sara did as he said, and three-quarters of an hour later she walked into the sitting room of their suite and stopped. Guido was not alone. An elderly couple had joined him. They were sitting on one of the sofas. A handsome white-haired man and an elegant woman with her hair swept up in a chignon, once a brunette but now with silver wings at the sides. Sara looked, and looked again…the woman seemed familiar.

'Good, Sara—you're ready.' Guido walked towards her, a strange smile on his face. 'You look beautiful.' She had dressed in a simple black dress with a low square neckline and was wearing the diamond necklace and earrings Guido had given her for her birthday.

'Who—' she started, but he cut her off by dropping a swift kiss on her open mouth.

'Sara.' He grasped her arm and let her towards

the couple. The man stood up, as did the woman, eyes fixed on Sara with such intensity she wondered if she had smudged her lipstick or something.

'I want you to meet Mr and Mrs Browning. Your grandparents.'

'What...?' Guido's arm curved around her waist to support her.

'It's true—I found them for you.'

And what followed was the most incredible evening of Sara's life.

Apparently it was now relatively easy in America to track down the donors, and that was what Guido had done. Unfortunately her father, Alexander Browning, was dead. He had died at the age of twenty, when on manoeuvres with his platoon in Africa. He was his parents' only son, and they'd been ecstatic when Guido had found them and told them about Sara. Amazingly, her grandfather Bob was an accountant in a small town in New England. And the reason his wife Laura looked familiar was because Sara was a younger image of her.

They dined and talked and swapped family stories until after midnight, and agreed to meet again the next day.

Much later, lying in the king-sized bed, sated from making love, Sara leaned on Guido's chest and looked down into his night-black eyes, her own filled with tears.

'Thank you for everything, Guido. It was a wonderful, unbelievable thing you did, looking for my father and finding my grandparents. You have made me the happiest woman in the world.'

'I aim to please,' he teased, smoothing the long tendrils of hair back from her face.

'Don't tease—I am serious.' A tear fell onto his broad chest.

'Oh, God—don't cry.'

'I'm not sad. These are tears of joy, because I love you so much, and under that hard exterior you are a big softie.'

'I'd do anything to keep you happy.' He grinned and wiped the tears from her cheeks. 'But a word of advice. It is not a good idea to call your husband a softie on his wedding night.

He might misconstrue your meaning and feel challenged to prove you wrong.'

Sara chuckled as she was taught the error of her ways.

MILLS & BOON PUBLISH EIGHT LARGE PRINT TITLES A MONTH. THESE ARE THE EIGHT TITLES FOR MAY 2008.

———————— ✍ ————————

THE ITALIAN BILLIONAIRE'S RUTHLESS REVENGE
Jacqueline Bair

ACCIDENTALLY PREGNANT, CONVENIENTLY WED
Sharon Kendrick

THE SHEIKH'S CHOSEN QUEEN
Jane Porter

THE FRENCHMAN'S MARRIAGE DEMAND
Chantelle Shaw

HER HAND IN MARRIAGE
Jessica Steele

THE SHEIKH'S UNSUITABLE BRIDE
Liz Fielding

THE BRIDESMAID'S BEST MAN
Barbara Hannay

A MOTHER IN A MILLION
Melissa James

MILLS & BOON
Pure reading pleasure

0408 Rom